"The Runaway Omega"

M/M Wolf Shifter Mpreg Paranormal Romance

Apollo Surge

Edition v1.00 (2019.06.21)
apollo@apollosurge.com

Special thanks to the volunteer readers who helped with proofreading. Thank you so much for your support.

Chapter One

Wes stopped short of the red house that he'd seen on his walks back into town. He didn't remember anything—at least geographically—from when he shifted, but he did remember having to go back, and this small cabin had always been an anchor for him when everything else had fallen into disarray.

He didn't want to do this, but he didn't think that he had much of a choice. The pack never went onto private property. It was too dangerous and they had lost too many people like that.

But Wes had to do this.

He needed the pack to stay away from him, and while he didn't think they'd lost his scent—because as Griffin had said to him, which still sent a shiver down his spine, everyone could smell him now —he knew that being in the house would be enough to stop them from coming for him.

At least for a month or two.

It was still spring, and things didn't really start for the pack until summer, but for his standing, his scent was powerful, and since he was one of the only omegas left in the pack... He shuddered as he hugged himself. He didn't want to think about it. He could feel himself starting to give in to his nature, especially when he was done shifting.

He always felt so empty after that. But the last thing that he wanted was to bring another Omega into his pack. He couldn't think of having his own child deal with what Wes was dealing with.

No wonder his father had left. He probably couldn't even deal with what would happen to Wes once he came of age. Or maybe he was just a terrible person, like the rest of the members of the pack said.

Wes didn't want to know. He couldn't have known, because even if he asked, Griffin never answered. He didn't think that Wes needed to know anything about his parenting lineage. If Wes had been more docile, which the pack had tried to instill into him, it might have worked.

But Wes was a new generation of Omega. He had grown up connected to the internet, and he had known that there were other choices for him out there.

At least that was what he wanted to believe.

He didn't know if it was true, but he was going to make it happen for himself, even if it meant that he had to claw his way out. Quite literally.

Now he was trying to get away from it all. Things weren't predestined, not necessarily, and the little red cabin at the edge of the woods might have been the perfect way to get away from them, at least until he came up with a more coherent plan.

A long-term one, in any case. He looked up at the red cabin and sighed. It was cold, and he could see his breath in front of his face.

This would be okay for the time being. Wes knew that he couldn't stay there for long, because the pack wouldn't take long to find him, and he didn't know how long they would respect the rule of not going onto private property. Probably only until they were all in heat.

He took a few steps forward and stopped short of the fence. It was a white fence, and it had been recently installed, but it was already dusty and covered in pollen. Wes only knew that it was new because he hadn't seen it in the last two years. It had only been there the last couple of months.

He thought that the house might have been sold, but he wasn't sure. Whoever used to live there didn't use to take nearly as much care of it as the new tenant.

This was a summer house, though, and he didn't think that whoever owned the property would be back for another month or so. Not until it got warmer. It was too cold up here for any city dwellers, though the place was beautiful when summer finally rolled around.

Vibrant and green with gorgeous lakes, it was perfect to get away from the world. The pack was subdued during summer, too, because the days were long and the full moon thing was a total myth. They needed their nights to be long and cold. That was when they went out to hunt and to frolic.

But the nights were getting shorter and the cusp of summer was when things went wild with the pack. It was when the lineage was supposed to continue.

It was when Wes was supposed to be claimed. A few weeks later, the next Omega would be born. Fast forward eighteen years—rinse and repeat, forever.

He had just come of age, and now he was supposed to fulfill his duty.

Fuck his duty, he thought as he held on to the white fence. It went against his instincts to jump a fence and to break into a house, because he thought that he might be found out and shot, but everything about this went against his instincts. Being away from his pack, trying to get away from his duty, it all seemed superhuman to him. It seemed right to him too.

He needed to do this.

He landed on the grass on the other side of the fence and exhaled heavily.

He closed his eyes, trying to get his heartbeat under control. The cabin was isolated enough that he didn't look around to see if anyone was watching him, but he didn't have to. His chief concern was doing this stealthily enough. He wasn't that worried about other people—other wolves—noticing him.

He would have been able to hear them, to smell them, in any case. And he would have known to run. But his pack was the only one for miles, and he could have easily recognized their smell and discern their footsteps.

All that he could hear was the sound of the forest, birds and squirrels and leaves brushing up against each other turning into mush in his head.

It was the middle of the day and his pack was still recovering from turning the night before. *He* was still recovering from turning, and from what Wes remembered from what people had told him in his pack, it was a bit like having a really bad hangover. His head was banging, his mouth was dry, and his eyes were watery, but he wasn't sure if that was from the cold or from the after-effects of turning.

He walked up to the white door and took a second to look at it. It had been recently painted, he noted, and whoever had painted it hadn't done such a great job of staying in the lines, though the job wasn't bad, exactly. It was more amateurish than bad, clearly done by someone who didn't spend a lot of time working with their hands.

He wondered what kind of person lived here. Hopefully, he would never have to find out. He would be long gone by the time the owner got to the cabin.

Maybe he would even get to go to the city. Somewhere warmer. He smiled, a little sadly, quite aware that it was never going to happen for him. Because of who he was, he was never going to be able to leave this remote corner of nowhere, was never going to get to live a normal life. Even being suburban—having children, a partner, a normal job—all seemed like completely remote possibilities to him.

No, not possibilities. Dreams. Impossible dreams.

He tried the handle. He knew better. He knew that it wouldn't work, but he couldn't help himself. That would have made his life a hell of a lot easier. But no, of course he couldn't just walk into the cabin. He moved the handle a little bit, but the door didn't budge.

Wes sighed and rested his head on the door. This was going to be harder than he thought. He stood back from the door and looked at the windows.

This wasn't going to be easy. The windows were double-glazed and they looked like they were sealed, so he wouldn't be able to pry them open with his fingers.

That didn't mean that he wasn't going to try.

He walked to the one closest to him, hearing little twigs break under him. He tried to place his hand under the ledge, but his fingers weren't small enough to get them in there.

He grunted.

Shit, the last thing that he wanted to do was blunt force this, but he was almost sure he didn't have much of a choice. Fuck. He swore under his breath as he looked at the red cabin.

He needed to decide which window would be easiest to break, which one wouldn't set off the alarm, if the owner had an alarm. Wes hoped that he didn't, but there was only one way that he was going to find out.

Upstairs was his best bet. He looked around, trying to find where it would be easiest to climb. There was a column holding up the porch, and though he didn't think it was going to be easy, it was the best option that he could ask for.

At least this way he could get away from the pack if he got into the cabin. He could finally escape.

He needed to make sure that he could get away with using the cabin as a getaway spot before he did anything else, though. He walked around the outside of the house and tried looking for a rock or a brick. While there were no bricks to be found, he finally found a big enough rock.

He picked it up, turned it around, and brushed the dirt and debris off it.

He took a deep breath, setting his gaze on the window right above him. He thought that he could make it. If he didn't make it, he was shit out of luck. He would have to rethink his entire strategy, maybe even where he was going to stay for the rest of the month.

The rest of the month was absolutely vital when it came to the rest of his life. He took a deep breath and threw the rock.

For a second, it looked like it was about to miss and stumble down onto the lip of the ceiling, and Wes wouldn't have been able to retrieve it. That would have been the worst, he thought. He could almost see it happening, too. But instead, it hit the target and when it came in contact with the window, it shattered it. It was the only thing that Wes could hear as the glass broke, little shards falling everywhere.

He took a step back, his eyes wide, and waited.

He was going to have to hide in the forest if he heard any sirens. He was ready for it, though he wasn't the most patient person in the world. He knew that it would take law enforcement a long time to get to the middle of nowhere, but they might be notified immediately. That was a risk he had to take.

He could get lost in the forest. He was an expert at getting lost.

He just wished that this hadn't taken so long, because the rest of the pack would be up soon, and they would be hunting for him.

He glanced at his watch and started to count down for ten minutes. By then, he should have heard sirens, even if only from afar. He didn't.

After a while, he opened his eyes again, and he started to climb up the column. His heart was beating fast. This was what he had to do, he was sure of it, but that didn't make it any easier.

He had never squatted in someone's house before, and he didn't intend for it to be a permanent solution. He had always had his own place, or at least his place with the pack. He would have to get used to it. If the choice was no child or a child born to the pack, then Wes's choice was no child. Definitely no child.

He climbed up the column and jumped onto the roof. He almost lost his balance, which would have been bad, but he managed to catch himself before he did. Slowly, he moved so that he was standing right outside the window.

He would have to replace the window, but he could do that later, after he had settled in. For the time being, he could cover it with a black garbage bag. He looked around the hallway but it was dark. He couldn't see anything, save for a few doors.

It didn't matter, though. He could take a closer look at the house once he had officially broken in. He took another deep breath and went into the hallway.

There was no sound from inside the house. He'd been lucky, he thought.

He fumbled around in the dark, looking for a light switch. After some searching, he found it. The hallway was small, but it was fine. It was what he needed. A house. A place to stay away from the pack.

He couldn't ask for much more.

As long as he had a place to stay, he didn't mind too much. He just couldn't stay out, because that meant he was unprotected from the elements and from his pack. The elements weren't too bad. It was his pack that worried him.

He decided that he would only stay there for a week. After that, he would have to find another place, probably one which was permanent. He couldn't squat in another person's house forever. That sounded like a horrible existence. He had a little bit of money saved but not much. It was money he had managed to grab from people's wallets when they weren't looking, because he didn't get any money. He didn't even get scraps.

He was just smart about it. He never took so much that anyone worried about the money that had gone missing. He'd been planning this for years, but it was still not enough to get a place that would fit his needs.

He didn't know where he could go where he would be able to shift, especially now that he was so close to being in heat. He was worried about that, but at least the first hurdle had been conquered.

He took a few seconds to collect himself, then he put his backpack down next to one of the doors. He needed to go downstairs and collect the garbage bag that was going to act as his window, along with some tape.

As he started walking downstairs, he finally managed to take a deep breath.

That was when he smelled it.

Shit.

The overwhelming musk that sent shivers down his spine, that made his mouth water, that made him pant. It was faint, but it was also all that he could concentrate on, because even though he could hardly sense it, he could feel it creeping into his lungs, into his blood.

This wasn't just a random cabin.

This cabin was owned by an alpha.

Chapter Two

When Joseph had decided to put his house in the city on the market, he hadn't expected it to sell for at least a few months. That would have given him enough time to shop around for another house with acreage, one that was far enough away from civilization that he could do everything that he needed to do without arousing suspicion, but close enough to the city that he could drive in and go into the office when he had to.

But the interested family had been insistent. More than insistent, they had been rich, and Joseph Turner was not the kind of man that walked away from a good deal.

Plus he had the cabin to go to. He'd only bought it a year ago and it still needed some work, but he was happy with it, and it would come in handy when the last of spring hit. He'd managed to smell the tail end of some wolves' scents the last time he'd been in town, but he didn't think that they ventured as far as his cabin.

He had also managed to convince his boss that he could work from home, that it wasn't necessary that he stay in the office, and that he could be just as productive when he was located somewhere remote. It had taken him about a year to get her to open up to the idea and he'd had to accelerate his finely tuned plans.

He'd been worried that it wasn't going to work and surprised when it had. The family wanted him to vacate the house as soon as he could, so he had collected his stuff, packed it all into his wagon, and decided to drive back to his cabin two weeks early.

Devin was curled up on the passenger seat next to him. Joseph looked at him and smiled. He had grown as much as he was going to and he was a good enough size that Joseph could get away with not living in smaller places because he had to look after his potbellied micropig.

Of course, when he'd first thought about it, the idea seemed ridiculous. He didn't want to take care of a pig and he didn't even like thinking about what would happen to the pig when he shifted.

But that was exactly what he needed to do, train himself so that he wouldn't attack anyone, and there was no easier way to do that than to acquire a pet that he cared deeply about and might eat in one of his alpha rages. Devin had grown to fifty pounds and he was a quirky enough pet that everyone thought Joseph was just a quirky person himself.

He smiled. They had no idea.

"Hey," he said to his pet pig as he stroked it. "We're almost home. You'll have a place outside. Don't worry, I brought you a sweater."

Devin looked at him with black, beady eyes and Joseph couldn't help but smile.

At least he wouldn't be completely alone, even if he felt like he might be going a little crazy. He knew that he would never find a life partner and a pet was... well, it was small consolation, but at least it was some consolation.

He stroked the pig's head and continued smiling. The fog had cleared up some and the drive had taken him a little less time than he'd been expecting, so he was going to have to figure something out for dinner. The place was so out of the way that he doubted he would be able to even order pizza.

He pulled up to the cabin and looked around. He didn't want to kill the ignition yet. He was always cautious when he got to new places, and the cabin was still a relatively new place for him.

He wasn't comfortable there yet. He probably wouldn't be comfortable there for a while. Not until he knew, for certain, that he was going to be okay.

This might even become his permanent home.

He just needed to make sure to try it out first, and not just for the summer. He leaned over, stroked Devin again, and Devin oinked at him.

"Stay in the car, okay, buddy? I'm going to have a look at the place. Make sure everything is on and working properly. I'll also turn on the heat so that you can be cozy when we're settled in."

Devin made a sound. That was enough to tell Joseph that he'd understood some of what he'd said. Devin was able to follow commands easily, because pigs were remarkably smart, and if Joseph told him to stay in the car, then he could almost be completely sure that Devin was going to do what he was told.

Joseph moved his hoodie so that it was over his ears, because it was freezing and he wanted to keep the cold off them. He stuffed his hands in his pocket, gripped his keys, and moved closer to the house.

Something was different.

He wasn't quite sure what it was, but... something.

He thought that it might be another wolf. It wasn't a pack, because a pack's scent would have been more overwhelming, and an alpha would have known to stay away from another alpha's territory.

He wasn't stupid. He knew better than to infringe on another alpha's territory. He had bought this cabin because he was sure that it was far enough away from any other wolf packs. That had been his intent from the beginning, and now...

Fuck. He took a deep breath, trying to steel himself. The scent got stronger the closer he got to the cabin, which made no sense to him. It shouldn't, in theory, be possible that there was another wolf here. He opened the door to his cabin and walked inside. He noticed how all of his hair was standing up on end, and he could feel his body start to tremble, his heart pounding in his chest.

"Hello?"

Nothing. No answer.

He knew that someone was in there, but they weren't answering. Another wolf. The last thing that Joseph wanted to do was get in a fight with another wolf. Shifting was always painful and Joseph had to be prepared before it happened.

His life was tightly planned around it so he hated when something like this happened.

This wasn't an alpha, though. It didn't smell like an alpha. It smelled like a wolf, certainly, but not a wolf that was a threat. The scent was familiar, and compelling, but Joseph couldn't be sure about it.

"Hello?" he said again, as he took another step toward his kitchen. He didn't think that anyone was going to say anything in return, but he couldn't stop himself from trying.

He could feel himself going into fight mode, but he fisted his hands at his sides and told himself to keep his cool. It was for just this sort of situation he had trained so hard.

Yes, it might have been going against every single one of his instincts, but that was something that he was more than well equipped for. It was the reason he had a pet that doubled as a snack. He was a good wolf.

He was a better person.

"I know you're there," he said, his voice echoing in his ears. "I'm not going to hurt you. I just need you to come out so I can see you, okay?"

He heard a whimper, but it wasn't nearby. Taking a deep breath, his arms close to his sides, he turned on his heels to go check in the pantry. It was big enough that a person could hide there, provided they weren't too big. It was also totally empty. He still hadn't gotten around to hanging up the shelves in there, so there was even more space than there would have otherwise been.

"Little wolf," Joseph said. "Come out. I won't hurt you."

He could smell the pheromones when he said that. It had partly been confirmation. He needed to make sure that the wolf in his house was an omega. If there had ever been any doubt, this dissuaded him from it. This was firmly an omega. He could smell it. He could feel it in his blood, flowing to the rest of him, going straight to his cock.

He swallowed. He needed to get a grip.

This might be an omega, but he was also a human being. He was a person.

"Hey," he said, his voice quiet, as he started to open the pantry door. "I'm not going to hurt you. I promise. You don't have to run. I just want to talk to—"

The moment that he had opened the door a couple of inches, he was knocked back. He was startled as he bumped into the back wall. He heard himself swearing under his breath.

Of course this was his fault. Joseph knew exactly why this had happened. It was because he was caught off-guard. He was trying so hard not to startle the person in his pantry, that he had failed to realize that he would be easy to take down if it came down to a confrontation. His nostrils flared. He was getting angry.

This person was in his house, not the other way around. Wolf or wanderer, whatever they were, whoever they were, they shouldn't have been in his house without asking.

"Hey!" he exclaimed. He took off running after the wolf. He didn't need to see the omega, which was lucky, because he had disappeared in a flurry and he had left Joseph behind as if he was some sort of inconvenience and nothing else.

It didn't matter, because Joseph could follow him with his nose. His scent was overwhelming enough to be able to do that and the guy had decided to go upstairs instead of outside for some inexplicable reason. He could smell the fear coming from the omega, coppery, a bit like blood.

He needed to find him and calm him down. Tell him that he wasn't interested in mating. This wouldn't be the first time that he would have to turn down an offer from an omega who had wandered away from his pack.

He followed the scent to the bathroom. The door was closed. The hallway upstairs was freezing, too, and it was only when he looked around that he realized that one of the windows had been broken. In its place was a garbage bag to seal the window, duct tape on his walls.

Joseph sighed and knocked on the door. "Hey," he said. "Seriously. I won't hurt you. I just want to talk."

He waited a few seconds, but there was no answer. He wondered how long the intruder would be able to hole himself up in there. He would have to come out soon, but soon could mean hours, maybe even days. Nights. He would have to come out to shift.

"Listen," he said. "If you don't come out and talk to me, I'm going to..."

What was he going to do? Blow and blow until the door came down? Turn and drag him outside by the scruff of his neck?

Nah. Those weren't options.

He closed his eyes. "If you don't come out, I'm going to call the police."

That seemed to garner some sort of response, though it appeared to take forever. He could hear shuffling and then steps coming toward him. The handle moved slightly, but the intruder seemed to think better of it and stopped himself from opening the door.

"Please don't do that."

"You're in my house," Joseph said. "You will understand why I don't feel safe."

"Spare me the bullshit," the deep voice replied. "Please. We both know I couldn't take you even if I tried. And I'm sure as hell not going to try."

"Okay. Well, like I said, I just want to talk. But I don't want to do it through a door."

The man seemed to consider this. "What guarantee do I have that you won't hurt me?"

Joseph sighed. "None," he said. "Nothing but my word. I promise you, I'm a man of my word."

"And why should I believe that?"

Joseph rolled his eyes. "Because you should, okay? You're the one who is in my house, hiding away from God knows what."

There was no answer for a second, which was enough to get Joseph to continue.

"This is where I live, in case you haven't noticed, and I still haven't called the police. If I was going to, I would have already done that. If I was going to hurt you, I would have already done that too."

"I guess," was the weak answer.

But it was enough. It was all that Joseph needed and it was clearly all that the man needed because he opened the door, slightly, just enough to show a little bit of his face.

There was not a lot of light, but Joseph could feel his heart jumping in his chest. He didn't think it was just his scent, though of course that didn't make him like the man any less. No, it was also the elongated shape of his nose, the sliver of his lips, the wide dark eyes with the curled eyelashes.

Little wolf, he caught himself thinking. He almost said it, but he knew better than that. This man was a stranger.

"I'm Joseph," he said to the man in the bathroom. "Joseph Turner."

"I'm... Wes."

Joseph smiled. "Okay," he said. "You don't have a last name, then?"

"I do," Wes said, opening the door. "I mean, I do have a last name. It's West. But people call me Wes."

Joseph could feel the crease in his brow. "Then what's your first name?"

Wes looked away from him. "I don't have one."

"You don't have a given name," Joseph repeated.

"If I do, I don't know what it is," Wes said. Then he shook his head. "I don't know why I'm telling you all this. You don't care."

Joseph tilted his head. He opened his mouth to say that he did care, but he didn't understand why he should care. He probably shouldn't. Yet there was something so magnetic about this guy... fuck, he wanted to take him in his arms, look into his eyes and tell him that everything would be okay.

But he didn't want to do that either, because he knew that was just his instinct. He knew that it was his instincts that made him want to be nice and protective toward this guy, but... there was something else about him that he couldn't help but like off the bat.

Something like a certain defiance. There was a fire in his eyes. One that he had never seen from an omega before, and it was making him feel things.

Things that he should probably not be feeling.

He tried to stop himself. This was stupid. He was being stupid. He needed to dismiss this guy, send him on his way. He wasn't going to call the police, because he could tell that the man was afraid, but he wasn't going to stand there and do nothing.

He didn't feel victimized. Wes was right. Joseph could easily take him, if he wanted to, but he didn't want to.

"Do you want a drink?" Joseph heard himself ask.

Wes looked at him. He blinked a couple of times, then he nodded. "You wouldn't mind?"

"Well, you're already here," he said. "It would hardly be an issue."

Wes thought about that for what Joseph felt was way too long, but the last thing that he wanted to do was pressure him. It was clear that he was having to think this through and Joseph was getting nervous.

He didn't really know what to expect from this guy and it was putting him on edge. He needed to know what to expect. He didn't like this. Having a drink with the guy would make it easier.

He would get a feel for him when they were drinking tea with each other. At least then Joseph would be able to pin him down. He would be able to make an informed opinion about this intruder.

Right now, all that he got were smells and his own nature, and that wasn't good. He was having to fight it, every step of the way, with every single thing that he said to Wes.

"Fine," Wes finally said.

Joseph tried to smile. He was still trying to be cautious, but there was something about this man that made him want to throw caution to the wind. He was magnetic. That was a problem.

Joseph walked down the stairs, but he let Wes go first. He didn't want to risk Wes going behind him and jumping out the window that he had broken, which was obviously how he had gotten into the cabin.

When he was walking down the stairs, Joseph hugged himself. After the excitement of finding an intruder in his house, that was all he had managed to think about. Now that the excitement had passed and he felt himself calming down, he noticed the environment around him.

It wasn't any warmer in the house than it was outside of it.

That was the first time that he realized it was still cold in the cabin, probably because this guy hadn't turned on the heat.

That concerned him, because it had been below freezing. Had he stayed in his bed? Had he bundled himself up and gotten under the covers in the guest bedroom?

He looked at his wide back as he wondered all of this. The guy was young. He hadn't seen his face that well, but he could tell that he was young from the way that he looked from behind as he walked away from him.

He could see his broad back, the way that his shirt looked painted on. He bit his lower lip as he resisted the urge to reach out and grab him. He knew better than that. Joseph knew better than to touch an omega—that was the easiest way to lose control, and he already felt so close to losing it.

Everything about this had thrown his carefully laid out plans into disarray.

"You haven't turned the heat on," he said when they got to the first floor.

Wes shrugged. "I don't want to make your heating bill go up. I figured I should try to make myself as invisible as possible."

Joseph regarded him for a while, wondering if he was telling the truth. "Do you mean you didn't want to make me suspicious?"

Wes sighed, rubbing the bridge of his nose. Though there wasn't much light, Joseph could feel the fear, the uncertainty. He could smell it in the air. He could see the hair on the back of Wes' neck standing up on end along with the hair on his arm.

Wes was still ready to bolt—or to fight, Joseph supposed, if it came to that. He wanted to assure him that it wouldn't, but the man had no reason to trust him.

Joseph closed his eyes. He needed to talk himself out of the idea that he was the one that was supposed to make this man feel better.

He was the one who had been victimized. He was the one who had walked into his house to find a stranger there, as if that was just a thing that he was supposed to have been expecting.

He was starting to get angry then, until he heard the quiet voice coming from Wes, who was also hugging himself, and who, it suddenly occurred to Joseph, must have been freezing his ass off.

"I guess. A little of both. I really did expect that I'd be gone by the time you got here."

Joseph softened the moment that he said that, though there was still an edge to his voice when he spoke. He didn't want Wes to think that he was okay with him simply crashing in his house without asking for permission. "Okay," he said. "And how long have you been here?"

Wes looked away from him, putting his arms around his chest, hugging himself close. "A few days," he said. "I didn't... I didn't expect you to be here so soon."

Joseph looked him up and down. "Were you going to rob me?"

Wes' eyes widened. He looked horrified by the very idea of that and Joseph couldn't help but wonder if he was a really good actor or if the thought had genuinely never occurred to him. "No," he said. "No, I was never going to rob you. I just needed a place to stay."

"How long?" Joseph asked, his eyes narrow.

"I don't know."

Joseph scoffed. "Don't I at least deserve the courtesy of your honesty, Wes?"

Wes bit his lower lip. "Yes," he said. "It's just—it's embarrassing."

"How about we have that cup of tea and you can tell me everything? I won't judge you," Joseph said. "I promise."

"You might."

"Well, I'll try hard not to," Joseph replied. "How does that sound?"

"Honestly? Like more than I deserve," Wes said. "Why are you being so nice to me? You're..."

He didn't need to say anything else. Joseph knew exactly what he was, just like Wes knew exactly what he was. Everything was going unspoken between them. Joseph wanted to know if Wes would try to deny it, maybe as a self-preservation measure.

"I'm not like the rest of them," Joseph offered. "Come to the kitchen. We'll turn the heat on, I'll go collect Devin from the car, and then we can talk."

"Devin?"

"Yeah."

"Is that your partner?"

"No, no. That's my pig. Devin Bacon."

Wes blinked. "Oh. Right."

"I'll be right back. Just gotta go turn that heat on."

Wes nodded, saying nothing.

Joseph could feel his gaze on him as he walked out the door.

Chapter Three

Wes was... confused. Afraid.

No, terrified.

But mostly confused. He was having a lot of feelings, none of which he could make much sense out of, because everything about this encounter had gone so differently from how he had expected. He had been sleeping when Joseph had arrived.

The last few nights had been uncomfortable. He had been alert, waiting for his pack to arrive, waiting for them to drag him back into the delipidated house they shared near the edge of town, close to nowhere. Wes had been right about none of them daring to go into private property, but they weren't in heat yet, and he didn't know how desperate they would get.

He was spent. If he hadn't been so tired, if he wasn't sleeping for the first time in what felt like weeks, then he was sure that he would have noticed.

He would have heard Joseph's vehicle on the road. He would have been able to smell an alpha coming from miles away. His nostrils were flaring when Joseph had arrived in the cabin, and he thought that he was just having a dream, especially because he was so hard that it almost hurt when he woke up. That happened before *the week,* as if his body was preparing him for it, but there was nothing to prepare him for.

Not in this particular case. He had gotten away from anything that he needed to have been prepared for. He was staying away from his pack, even if he felt the pull of returning, even if he felt his body betraying him in the most basic of ways.

He didn't like to think what his life would be like right now if he had stayed with his pack. At least there was the small consolation that it would probably be worse than getting caught by the alpha.

So far, he didn't seem too bad. Not for an alpha, in any case. Of course Wes could smell him on the sheets, in the toiletries left in the bathroom, on the towels—but the smell was faint, slowly wiped away by time, and Wes had, mistakenly, thought that he wouldn't be back for another few weeks yet.

At least not until the season was over.

But the season hadn't really started and Wes couldn't help but shudder at the thought of spending the season with this alpha. He wondered if the alpha was going to try and give him a choice—his pack or him.

He didn't think so, because he didn't seem like the kind of alpha that would enforce that, but the season hadn't really happened yet and Joseph might be the kindest, nicest person in the world and the worst wolf ever. When a wolf was in heat, no one could ask him to be reasonable.

No one could ask him to be anything. No one could ask for anything from them, because they were nothing but animals. They were simply there to follow their biological imperatives.

Their top most biological imperative was to procreate.

He shuddered as he thought about that.

Maybe he would be able to get away from Joseph soon enough too.

He just needed to plan it. He needed to decide how he would be able to get away from him and then plan it, seriously plan it, so that it didn't fall on the same night that the season started.

The last thing that he wanted was to be caught by the pack when he was trying to escape from them, especially on one of the nights when they would already be in heat.

He didn't even want to think about facing that prospect. There were five of them, only one of him, and he didn't like thinking about fighting them off.

With one alpha, well, he didn't feel like he was going to be good at it, but at least there was something of a chance. Joseph would be stronger and faster than him, but Wes was smart and resourceful and… maybe he wouldn't even have to defend himself from Joseph.

Hadn't Joseph said that he was going outside to get a pig? Wes wondered what he'd meant.

Joseph walked back inside and Wes looked up, his jaw dropping open. Joseph had been speaking plainly, which was apparent from the pig wearing the Christmas sweater that he was holding in his arm.

"He would never forgive me if I made him stay out for too long," Joseph said.

"Right."

"You don't believe me? Pigs never forgive."

Wes tilted his head. "Okay."

"Anyway, hold on. Let me just get him settled and then I'm all yours."

Wes nodded. "Sure."

Joseph smiled at him. It was the first time that Wes had seen him smile, and he couldn't help but stare a little when he did. Joseph was a good-looking man, that much was obvious just from taking a cursory look at him. But there was something about the way that his face looked when he smiled. His eyes lit up and his teeth—fuck, there was something about his smile, about his slightly crooked teeth, about his canines.

He closed his eyes.

No, this wasn't—this wasn't him. This wasn't a part of himself that he wanted to listen to.

This was the part of himself that was drawn to Joseph, to the lifestyle, to his pack. The very thing that he was trying so desperately to run away from.

He closed his eyes and took a deep breath. He heard Joseph doing some things, though he didn't want to open his eyes to see what they were. He knew that there was no way that he could outrun an alpha, so he wasn't going to try.

He would have to plan his next move carefully.

"How do you take your tea?" Joseph said.

Wes opened his eyes and looked around the kitchen. He saw Devin Bacon in the corner of the room, bundled up in what looked to Wes like a dog bed and a couple of blankets to cover his curly tail. The front of his body was covered with a Christmas sweater so he would have been nice and warm without the help of any of the blankets, but it was clear that Joseph was a careful pet owner.

Or he really liked playing with his food.

"Wes?"

"I don't know," Wes said. "I've never really… had tea."

Joseph watched him for a second, then he nodded. "Of course," he said. "I'll make it how I make it for myself, then you can decide how you like it. How does that sound?"

Wes nodded. "Sounds okay."

"Good," Joseph said. "So normally, I have a little tea and a little sugar. Picked up the habit from when I studied in England. Really helps with the cold."

Wes watched him as he walked over to the stove, put the kettle on, grabbed two cups out of the cupboard and then grabbed two teabags from the cupboard above the sink.

He wiped them with the edge of his shirt. "You haven't used the kitchen?"

"I told you," Wes said. "I didn't want to inconvenience you. Any more than I had to."

"You really did think that you were going to crash here until I was gone?"

"Yes," Wes said. "You have to understand. I'm not homeless..."

He trailed off when he said that. He supposed that he was homeless. That was the easiest, most accurate way to describe his situation.

"I guess I am. I'm sorry," he said. "I'll be out of your way soon. Just need to get my stuff. I have enough to repay you for the window and—"

"Wait," Joseph said. "Stay. I've already put the tea on, so really, you might as well. It's freezing out there and I'm willing to bet money that you don't have a vehicle to drive away in. Otherwise, I don't think you'd be here in the first place."

Wes nodded. It was clear that Joseph could read him extremely well. He didn't know if that was because he was an alpha, or if it was because he was the kind of man who could just read people. Wes was a particularly easy target, because he wore his emotions on his sleeve.

It was something that his pack had frequently made fun of him for, and he couldn't see a way around it, though it would have been unfair to say that he hadn't tried.

Wes had definitely tried.

He had tried to practice, so that it wasn't as obvious that he was upset, but they teased him mercilessly even when he gave himself slightly away, so he let it go. It didn't matter if he tried, anyway. At least that was what the pack said.

They said it was in his nature. That because he was an Omega, he couldn't fight it, he couldn't pretend that he wasn't emotional and vulnerable. He had stopped trying, then, and he was sure that it showed, even to a stranger like Joseph.

Because Joseph might have been a stranger, but he was also an alpha, so he could probably read Wes extremely easily.

Wes nodded. "Yeah, I don't have a car. But still, you don't have to take pity on me."

"I disagree," Joseph said. "Pity is working very much to your advantage right now."

Wes smiled, a little dryly. "I guess that's the truth."

"So tell me," Joseph said. He was finishing up the tea. He walked over to where Wes was, and Wes took it, smiling at him gratefully. His hands had been cold, but now they were warming up, and his entire body was grateful because the central heating had started to kick in.

"Tell you what?"

"About you," Joseph said. "Why are you here?"

Wes swallowed.

"You don't have a pack? Are you trying to find an alpha? Because if you are, you should know that I—"

"No," Wes said, holding his hand up to stop him. "No, I'm not looking for a new alpha, and I'm not looking to sleep with you."

"I didn't say anything."

"You might as well have, Joseph," Wes said, sighing impatiently. He brought the tea to his lips, took a sip and felt the sweet warmth in his mouth. "This is good."

He closed his eyes and took another sip. Joseph watched him for what felt like a very long time, but it turned out that the tea was exactly what he needed.

It made him feel less adrift, like maybe everything was going to be okay.

Or like maybe he was only so paranoid because he'd been hungry. He had been living off scraps lately, cutting corners, and he was almost down to his last slice of bread.

He hadn't realized just how much something warm and homey would help him. He finished it all, wiped his mouth with the back of his hand, and sat back in his chair.

"Thank you for the tea," Wes said.

"You're welcome. How was it?"

"It was… good," Wes said, closing his eyes. "It reminded me of something, though honestly, I can't remember what."

"Good," Joseph replied. "I'm glad you liked it. Would you like some more?"

"No," Wes said. "I feel a little lightheaded. I think that's the most food I've had in a little while."

"That's not food," Joseph said, clearly scandalized.

Wes felt a tug at the corner of his lips. He had heard of nurturing alphas, but as far as he knew, they were all myths. Omegas getting together at the end of a horrible day and trying to make themselves feel better told each other stories of sweet, nurturing alphas, stories of alphas that weren't real and only existed in the imagination of omegas who were fed up with the abuse they were subjected to every day.

There was no way that Wes could blame them, but he knew better than to believe in fairytales.

He wasn't an idiot.

He knew that the man whose house he had decided to crash in might be very nice to him right now, but that didn't mean that he was always going to be nice to him.

His ability to be sweet had an expiration date. Still, Wes could see the pull of believing it, the idea that this sweet and good-looking man might not want anything from him after all.

He doubted it. He knew better than to believe it. He still felt the pull of it. It was a very tempting lie. It was a comforting lie, the kind that he could wrap himself with like a blanket, the kind that he could see himself believing because it was good. Because it was convenient.

But convenient wasn't true. Wes knew that. He knew it from experience, knew it from the fact that he could feel his body reacting to his alpha and knew that the alpha would be reacting too.

He would be able to feel it in his body. He would be able to feel it in his core, even if he was trying to get away from it all.

"Wes," Joseph said, bringing him back to the here and now. "What are you trying to do?"

"What do you mean?"

"By staying here," Joseph replied. "What are you doing in my house?"

Wes bit his lower lip, his gaze darting away from Joseph's. He didn't think that he would be able to look right at him when he answered. He fisted his hands up next to him. "I'm just trying to get away from my pack, that's all."

Joseph nodded. Wes could see his movement from the corner of his eye.

"They won't come onto private property?"

Wes shook his head. "I'm sorry."

"It's okay," Joseph said. "Do you mind if I ask you about them?"

Wes' eyes widened, his heart beating fast in his chest. He had heard of alphas taking over packs before. He was only trying to get away from his pack, he wasn't trying to harm them. If Joseph went after Griffin...

"I just want to know so I can be prepared if they come over here."

"Don't worry," Wes said. "I'll be long gone before they come here."

"Even then," Joseph replied. "I imagine that finding another alpha so close near their territory won't be something they tolerate very well. You know that they're not going to just go looking for you, they'll be able to track you here."

"They won't come inside," Wes offered.

"Maybe when they're not in heat," Joseph said. "You have to tell me what they're like so that I can be prepared. You know one of us could end up dying if you don't."

Wes glowered at him. He was probably being dramatic, because it wasn't as if this was a hundred years ago and they were barbaric, but he got what Joseph was trying to say.

Not telling him who his pack was would put both his pack and Joseph in danger, especially if Joseph was stupid enough to challenge Griffin when he came over looking for his omega.

"Okay," Wes said. "Fine. That makes sense."

"Good," Joseph said. "So more tea?"

Wes shook his head.

"Then you won't mind if I get some for myself."

"No, of course not," Wes replied. "Go ahead, please."

Joseph nodded. He got up, served himself some tea again, and brought it to his lips. He had a small beard and Wes couldn't help but watch him, wondering if he was wetting his beard when he was drinking his tea.

"I'm listening," Joseph said.

Wes nodded. "I don't know what you want to know."

"Everything," Joseph replied. "Everything that you can think of. Let's start with why you're here. You're an omega, so surely you're highly prized by your pack?"

Wes shook his head. "I mean, I guess in a way I am. Just for what I can do I am, but I don't want this."

"What don't you want?"

Wes sighed again. He could feel his eyes getting filled with tears as he started to speak. He was almost positive that Joseph would tell him to stop being such a baby, that he needed to suck it up and fulfill his purpose as an omega.

But Joseph didn't say anything. He was watching him, "I don't want to have to live as a being in service of the other wolves in my pack."

Joseph blinked. "Huh?"

"What?"

"I don't know," he said. "Your experience is clearly very different from mine."

Wes shook his head and scoffed. He looked away from Joseph when he answered. He didn't want Joseph to see just how deeply this was affecting him, exactly how upset he was about it all. "I don't want my child to have the life I had."

He hoped that would be enough for Joseph to let it go. He hoped that it would be enough for him to understand exactly why he had decided to smash a window and use his summer cabin as a place to hide away from his pack.

But the silence wasn't empty and it was clear to Wes that Joseph wasn't satisfied when he looked up at him again.

"Look," he said, wiping his tears from his eyes and feeling like an absolute idiot. "I get it."

Joseph watched him. "What do you get?"

Wes scoffed again. "I understand that it's my biological imperative to carry a child to term."

Joseph said nothing to that, but he didn't need to.

Wes was getting a little too riled up to be stopped by the way that Joseph was looking at him.

He waved his hands in front of his face. "Look, I get it. I'm supposed to be the omega and be there for the rest of the pack so that I can carry their children."

Joseph's eyes widened. "That's how they do it in your pack?"

"That's not how they do it in yours?"

Joseph licked his lips, but Wes noticed that he declined to answer. He was curious about the alpha's pack, but he supposed if he didn't want to talk about it, he couldn't force him.

After all, he was the one that had been caught in Joseph's house. He didn't have the right to ask any questions, because he didn't get any privileges. His status as both an intruder and an omega made it so that he was the lesser of the two of them, regardless of how praised his position was.

"I came here because I needed to get away from them," he said, his voice a whisper.

"Before the season started?"

Wes nodded, the tears in his eyes sliding down his cheeks. God, he hated this. He was exactly what Griffin said he was. Useless and always showing his hand. He sniffled a little and wiped his tears with the back of his hand.

"It's okay," Joseph said. "You're safe here."

Wes glared at him, but then Joseph extended his hand, and he patted Wes' own. That was it. That was all that it took to get him from crying a little bit to crying like a bitch, which was exactly what he wanted to avoid.

Before he could stop himself, he was sobbing. It was embarrassing and he wished that he could stop it, but it was as if everything that he had been bottling up for the last few years was coming out.

He knew that there was a chance that Joseph might use it against him, but right then he didn't care that much.

All that he cared about was getting it off his chest. He was sobbing, great big sobs, his shoulders moving up and down, as if he was a child.

The only thing that he could hear apart from his own pathetic sobs was the pig, and the heat, and the way that it was shaking the walls of the house. He couldn't help but draw a comparison between himself and the house, though he knew that it was stupid.

By the time he was done, his eyes hurt, his nose hurt, and his throat hurt.

Joseph was watching him curiously, saying nothing still. Wes waited.

He wasn't sure what he was waiting for. Part of him thought that he was waiting for Joseph to tell him to man up, that this wasn't a big deal, that he needed to grow the fuck up.

But Joseph continued saying nothing. Instead, he stood up, walked over to his suitcase, opened it, and rummaged in there for something that Wes couldn't see.

He could see the edges of a smile from his profile. He wondered what he was doing and couldn't help but be a little concerned, but when he turned around, he held a white cotton handkerchief

"From when I first started knitting," he said. "But that was when my eyes were better. I made this scarf. But then I realized I'm better at something like crochet, because my fine motor skills just aren't there for this."

Wes blinked. "Wow."

"What? Not good enough?"

Wes shook his head, taking the handkerchief and looking at it. "It's really beautiful, actually. Did you seriously do this?"

"Why is that so hard to believe?"

"My alpha—"

"No," Joseph said. "The alpha you know."

Wes shrugged. He couldn't see that much of a difference. "He's nothing like this," he said. "He would never do anything this beautiful, this delicate."

Joseph smiled, though the smile didn't quite reach his eyes. "It's been hard to train myself to be the person I want to be. I've had to do things like see the beauty in small things. I've learned to really love crafting things, knitting things, making small things."

Wes watched him.

"Long story short, it helped me when I needed to get away from my own pack."

Wes smiled at him. Maybe he did understand, even if he didn't understand completely. Maybe he got it a little bit.

"I'm sorry about that," he said. "I didn't mean to be such a weepy mess in front of you."

"It's okay," Joseph said. "You've only been away for a little bit. It must still be really hard for you."

"It's... an adjustment," Wes replied.

Joseph nodded. "I get it," he said. "Trust me."

"You do?"

Joseph looked around him. "There's no one else here, is there?"

Wes smiled at that. "Yeah, I guess not," he said, sniffling again. He was done crying, but he had already broken down in front of this guy, and being vulnerable didn't seem so bad anymore. It was clear that he had made a fool of himself in front of Joseph and things couldn't get that much worse. "My father left when I was little and I've been trained all my life to do this."

"Right."

Wes shook his head. "It's not right, Joseph," he said. "It's anything but right."

"Why?"

"Because these are all wolves that I'm related too," Wes said, looking away from Joseph, his hands fists at his side. "I don't know who impregnated my father though I'm pretty sure it was our current alpha, Griffin."

There was a long silence, a pause, as Joseph absorbed this information. "Oh."

"And then I'm supposed to just have another baby, and he can be the omega when he gets to eighteen, and I don't know if I'm okay with that."

Joseph closed his eyes. "I'm sorry," he said. "That sounds really hard. The rest of your pack?"

"Betas," Wes said, waving his hand in front of his face. "They, um, have a turn. After Griffin."

"Your alpha."

"Yeah," Wes said.

"Jesus, Wes... that sounds horrible."

"It's okay," he said, shrugging his shoulder. "I mean, I'm not afraid of the prospect of it. I just don't want to bring a child into it. I'm... I don't want a child to be trained by the same people, so that he has to be impregnated by them when he gets to be my age."

Joseph blinked. "Wouldn't you also maybe give birth to an alpha?"

Wes furrowed his brow. He hadn't thought about that, not really, but now that Joseph said it, it made sense. How else was there going to be an alpha to take over when Griffin died?

Wes shrugged. "I've been told that the omega only ever gives birth to omegas."

Joseph cocked his head. "That's a lie."

"Yeah," Wes said, licking his lips. "Yeah, I just figured that out."

"You might have siblings you don't know about."

Wes nodded. "Yup, that's probably right," he said. "I... I feel like an idiot."

"It's okay," Joseph said. "You're supposed to trust your pack. I get it."

Wes trained his gaze on Joseph. "Were you exiled too?"

Joseph chuckled, a little dryly, then shook his head. "No," he said. "I left when I came of age. Kind of like you."

Wes watched him, his eyes narrow. "And what have you done since?"

Joseph took a second to think about that. "I don't know," he said. "Lived."

"Okay," Wes said. "Thank you for the tea, I'll—"

"No," Joseph said. "You can stay."

Chapter Four

Joseph wasn't sure what had gotten into him. He should have known better, but when Wes was in front of him, crying openly, telling him how horrible his pack was, Joseph couldn't bear the idea of sending him back to the people that were so eager to hurt him.

Because that was what they were doing.

Joseph remembered what it had been like in his pack. It had been about five years since he had left, and he could remember everything as if it had happened only a few days ago. Wes would have felt safe with Joseph's pack, because their philosophy was very different from the philosophy that Wes' pack seemed to have.

But even when the omega was treated like a precious gem by the rest of the pack, there was something about the whole thing that had rubbed Joseph the wrong way since the very beginning.

The boy who was supposed to be his omega felt like a brother to him. They had been raised alongside each other since they were very little. They had played together when they were little boys, talked about their crushes when they were teenagers, dared each other to do stupid things when they were a little older. They had learned to drive alongside each other, gotten each other drunk more than once, held each other when crying as their parents started fading, as they passed away.

They were close. They shifted together too and talked about it, and then they shifted together again. Then Maurice had fallen in love with a girl at the gas station, right before either one of them came of age, and Joseph had been expected to get him pregnant.

The very thought of having sex with Maurice made Joseph feel sick to his stomach.

It made Maurice feel sick to his stomach too, Joseph was sure of it. Then he had come of age, and he had turned, and he could vaguely remember chasing Maurice through the woods.

He remembered cornering him, a gray wolf with white patches, looking luminescent against the dark of night. He was bigger than him, stronger than him, faster than him—he just needed to bite his neck, get him to submit, then he could drag him back to the barn and wait for him to turn again.

He couldn't remember any thoughts from that moment, but he could remember his instincts. His instincts were to grab Maurice, to hurt him, to make him feel Joseph everywhere, including inside of him.

He remembered what he thought about it after he turned, when he had dragged him back to the barn by the scruff of his neck, Maurice whimpering alongside him, his snout close to the ground. He had submitted to Joseph, just the way that he was supposed to, and when they got to the barn, Joseph was supposed to wait for him to turn before he had him.

But when Maurice had turned, Joseph could see the tears in his eyes, and despite the hormones raging inside of him, he couldn't go through with it.

He couldn't do that to his best friend. He couldn't do that to his brother. He just couldn't, no matter what his body was telling him, despite the fact that he was so hard that it was hurting him.

It wasn't who he was. He wasn't going to have sex with Maurice and watch him cry as he did it, because he was pretty sure that it would end with him crying himself. The whole thing seemed barbaric to him. He ignored his raging hard on and sat at the side of the barn while Maurice panted, clearly ignoring how turned on he was too. The two of them were far enough away from each other that they couldn't physically engage, which was good because if they had, Joseph would have probably ended up fucking Maurice despite neither one of them wanting it to happen.

They had talked about their childhood. Swimming in the lake when it was just kissed by a ray of sunshine and still cold. Running in the mud until their shoes were covered in filth. Talking to each other through scary nights when other wolves were coming for their things, as the rest of their pack stayed outside and fought them off.

They had fallen asleep at opposite sides of the barn. When he had woken up, at the crack of dawn, when the rest of the pack was circling them, he had decided that he had to leave.

He couldn't stay there and wait for his nature to take over his good sense. He had run away when they were still trying to look for them, when they were trying to see the aftermath of what was supposed to be the first night of mating.

He didn't regret running away. He had known that it was the right thing to do back then and he didn't think that he would make a different decision now. He didn't think that it was possible not to miss his family, because of course he did, but mostly he was glad that he wasn't expected to have sex with people that might or might not be related to him anymore.

They were never very clear about that in his pack and he was absolutely positive that it was not his place to ask. He had left then and hadn't looked back. It had been the right decision for him.

He couldn't help but see a little bit of himself in Wes. He was defiant. He didn't want to do what he had been tasked to do all his life. The most important part—the part that endeared him to Wes probably way more than it should have—was the way he was so resolutely against doing anything which might harm someone that he ended up bringing into this world.

There was something about that. Something that made Wes seem strongly moral and right, though it was clear to Joseph that there was a chance that Wes was afraid for his life.

The last thing that Joseph wanted to do was to take advantage of Wes, or to make Wes feel like he had to go to a pack of abusive wolves that would undoubtedly get him to submit in no time. His fighting spirit would be lost and that would certainly be a shame.

He supposed that was the reason that he had told Wes that he could stay with him. He had done it before thinking it through, because the complications that Wes staying with him carried were too many to count, but for the time being, it seemed right.

It was very likely that they were going to have to find other accommodations for him before the season really started, but for the time being, he could crash there, at least until he felt safer. That was what Joseph told himself.

He was a temporary stop for a little wolf who still needed to find his place in the world, so Joseph wasn't going to kick him out and he wasn't going to prompt him to leave. That would have been cruel. At least until he was ready to go.

Joseph closed his eyes.

Wes was still in the kitchen while Joseph got his stuff out of his bag.

He could hear Wes playing with Devin, laughing as his pig snorted.

He couldn't help but smile at the sound, which somehow seemed oddly familiar, despite the fact that he was positive that he had never heard it before in his life.

He couldn't be mad at Wes. He wanted to, because that seemed like the perfect defense mechanism, but he couldn't.

He got it.

Yeah, Wes had broken his window and stayed in his house without permission which Joseph didn't appreciate, but he got it. He understood what the little wolf was going through.

When Joseph had first been away from his own pack, it had been really difficult to have a life away from other wolves. He didn't understand human society that well and it was hard for him to step into a role where he had to earn money and live among people who didn't understand shifters and who thought that they were a myth.

He wanted the transition for Wes to be a little smoother. He understood that what Wes was going through had to be, by its very nature, harder than what he had been going through.

His very nature was to feel a pull toward his alpha, and the fact that he had managed to overcome it without any training filled Joseph with a certain sense of awe.

Even Maurice had been begging him to do it that night after they'd shifted, though there were tears streaming down his face. He didn't want to see anyone have to go through that again and it was clear to him that Wes was a sensitive guy.

He didn't want him to have to go through that at all, not if he could help it.

Once he had finished putting his clothes away, it was time to go downstairs. He had wanted to give the two of them some space from each other so that they could both think through what was happening. Joseph knew that he needed to have some rules in place before he let Wes stay, including a hard deadline for when he had to leave.

There was also the upcoming season.

He shuddered a little, though he wasn't cold anymore. He wondered how that was going to be. He wasn't looking forward to this conversation, that was all that he knew for sure.

He was wearing jeans and a long-sleeved shirt because he was almost sure that he would have to go get food from town again and that was a good thirty minutes away. He wanted to get into his pajamas but there was absolutely no way that he was going to let Wes stay in his house when he wasn't there.

He walked downstairs and into the kitchen. He found Wes sitting next to a curious and happy looking Devin, who was oinking at him.

"Hey," he said.

Wes looked up at him for a second, then back at Devin. His cheeks had gone red and he was focusing on Devin again. "Hey," he replied.

"Sorry I took so long," Joseph said. "I was just unpacking some stuff."

Wes shrugged. "It's okay," he said. "It's your house."

Joseph smiled at that, though he could hear the apprehension in Wes' voice.

"I'm not going to kick you out."

"I didn't say that you were going to," Wes said. "But I don't know. I wouldn't be mad if you did. I would get it."

"I know," Joseph said. "But that's not what I want. We do need to talk, though."

Wes nodded. "Yeah."

Joseph cocked his head. "Where have you been sleeping so far?"

Wes looked away from him.

"I couldn't smell you on my bed..."

"The bathtub," Wes said.

Joseph's eyes widened. "You've been sleeping in the bathtub?"

Wes nodded. "I thought that would make it harder for you to know that I was around," he said. "You know, when you got back."

Joseph blinked. "How... weren't you uncomfortable?"

Wes shrugged. "Small sacrifice to pay for staying in your house and not paying a penny."

Joseph shook his head. "We need to make things clear."

Wes watched him, saying nothing.

"How about we go get some pizza or something? It'd be nice to have dinner in a neutral territory."

Wes' eyes widened. "I can't go back to town. I can just leave, if—"

Joseph shook his head again. He was embarrassed at his stupid oversight. "Of course," he said. "How about we order some Chinese food or something? It might take a little while but..."

The smile on Wes' face made Joseph quiet down immediately. He would have waited days if it meant that he would see Wes smiling like that.

"Okay," Joseph said, smiling at him. "Let me know what you want."

"I've never had Chinese food."

"Really?"

Wes nodded. "I ate what Griffin hunted."

"So you've never had any... human cooked food?"

Wes shook his head. "Not as far as I know."

"Okay," Joseph said. "We're going to fix that."

He looked him up and down.

"I mean, we're going to... to fix all of this," Joseph added, more to himself than to Wes. Wes watched him, saying nothing, and for a second, Joseph wondered if he had offended him.

He hadn't intended to, but he would understand if Wes was angry at his words then.

But Wes just nodded, as if what he had said made perfect sense. Of course they needed to fix this. He was glad that Wes agreed, because he didn't know if he would have been able to cope with it otherwise.

"Listen to me," Joseph said, surprised by the intensity in his own voice. "We're going to make sure that you never have to do anything you don't want to do. Do you understand? We're going to make it so that you live the life you want. I promise."

Wes looked at him with wide eyes. He opened his mouth to say something, but then he clamped his lips shut, and Joseph continued staring at him, half-waiting for him to say that he was wrong, that he couldn't say anything like that, but he didn't.

He was quiet. Then he nodded and Joseph couldn't help but melt a little bit. He couldn't believe how much Wes had let him in in such a quick time, and part of him was still a little hesitant, because this was all still a bit much.

Every time that he closed his eyes, he still thought about the fact that Wes had already been in his house when he had walked in.

He opened his eyes and found Wes smiling at him, but there was a question in his eyes.

"I'm still getting used to this," Joseph said.

Wes shook his head. "You don't have to get used to it, Joseph," he said. "I'm not your responsibility."

"No," Joseph replied. "But you're here, so I might as well help."

Wes' smile turned into a grin.

***

Joseph couldn't help but smile when he saw Wes gobbling up the Chinese food. He had finished a huge serving of food, rice and noodles, along with steamed vegetables, sweet and sour chicken, lo mein beef—Joseph had thought that the food was going to last them for at least a couple of days, but he hadn't anticipated just how hungry Wes would be.

He didn't mind feeding him, especially because it was clear to Joseph that he had been undereating for God knew how long. Joseph didn't like to think about it very much.

It was interesting and also kind of sad to watch Wes eat, when he kept those things in mind. He was starving and he ate like the food was going to be yanked away from him any second. It greatly upset Joseph to think that Wes ever went hungry, that someone was ever anything but kind to him.

Wes struck him as the kind of wolf—the kind of person—who tried to be kind even when people weren't being kind to him.

Wes licked his lips and his eyes rolled to the back of his head. He made a sound which was slightly sexual and Joseph cleared his throat, reminding himself that the man in front of him was completely off limits.

There was no way that Joseph was going to have sex with Wes. Doing that would undermine everything that Wes was trying to do. Joseph thought that he had enough control to make sure that didn't happen, but he knew that he would have to take other measures to prevent anything from happening between the two of them.

Joseph might have been trained but Wes wasn't.

Wes grabbed the can of soda from in front of him, brought it to his lips, tilted his head back and sighed happily once he was done.

He burped and put his hand in front of his mouth, mumbling a weak, "Pardon me," when he did.

Joseph turned to smile at him and to tell him that it was no big deal, but Wes' eyes were still glued to the plate in front of him, which was now empty, and he seemed to be wondering something.

There was a sadness in his eyes too and Joseph couldn't help but clamp his hand over Wes' shoulder. Wes looked at him and smiled.

"Thank you," Wes said, his voice a hoarse whisper.

Joseph nodded. This reminded Joseph of the fact that Wes had never had human food in his life, that he really didn't understand what the human way of life was like.

He got it. He understood what being in an isolated pack was like, but this was too much.

It was clear that Wes' pack had tried to hide him from the rest of the world so that their one and only omega wouldn't escape, and that very fact made his stomach churn.

Clearly it made Wes' stomach churn too or he wouldn't be there.

"I'll help you clean up," Wes said. "Thank you, seriously. For, uh, everything. Not just for the food."

Joseph watched him.

"I mean it," he said. "You could have just kicked me out the moment you found me in your house. You could have called the police or..."

They both knew what Joseph could have done. Wes didn't have to say it. It was on both of their minds. Joseph shook his head. "I would never do that," he said.

"I know," Wes replied. "But I didn't know when I first came in here."

"I know you didn't," Joseph said. "Is it wrong to say that I'm glad you stayed?"

Joseph knew that he shouldn't have said that. He knew that everything between them was temporary, if there was even anything between them. He couldn't let himself feel that there was, just because their circumstances happened to align and put them in the same place at the same time.

Once they were done cleaning up and the kitchen was spotless, it was time to discuss what was going to happen over a cup of coffee. They needed to get some boundaries in place, especially for when the two of them started shifting, but they were putting off the conversation, probably because it was an uncomfortable conversation to have.

Once Joseph had finished showing Wes how to work the French press and Wes drank his coffee—apparently, it was the one thing that he did drink—the two of them sat at the plastic table in the kitchen while Devin snored away in his little knitted sweater and under his quilt.

It was all so perfectly domestic that it was hard for Joseph to remember why he was there in the first place.

"So," Joseph said, taking the last of his coffee. "We need to talk about... you know, how things are going to work."

Wes nodded.

"There are some rules in my house, Wes. You should know that."

Wes swallowed, looking away from him. His cheeks were a deep dark red. "I know," he said. "I'll replace your window as soon as possible."

Joseph nodded. "Sure," he said. "That's great. Do you have money?"

Wes watched him, saying nothing.

"Windows are expensive," Joseph explained. "Getting someone here to replace it is going to be even more expensive than the window."

Wes rubbed the bridge of his nose. "I can install the window," he said. "I'm handy."

Joseph nodded. "Okay," he replied. "What about the window itself?"

Wes continued to look away from him, saying nothing for a little bit.

Joseph didn't want to prompt him. He didn't want to accidentally make him feel like he was demanding payment, because he wasn't. He didn't care about the window. He only cared about establishing a set of rules for both of them, so that neither one of them fell into a trap about the other one.

He could easily see that happening.

He could see it happening because he hadn't been able to stop looking at Wes, though he should have. He hadn't been able to stop looking at the way that Wes' eyes lit up every time that their gazes locked. He could see the way his pupils expanded and his gaze darted down to Wes' lips and he couldn't help but wonder if he tasted just as good as he smelled.

"I have a little bit that I saved up before I left," Wes said, mercifully bringing Joseph out of his trance. Maybe it was an omega thing, but Joseph couldn't be sure.

On the other hand, he hadn't felt this way about anyone else. Joseph had *dated*. He had made sure to date and to sleep around, because that was the easiest way to learn to control himself.

No human wanted to see the animalistic part of him and if there was one thing that was drilled into his head ever since he was a cub, it was that he had to keep the existence of their species a secret.

That, other than mating, was the biological imperative.

So he'd gotten a mini pig, and he'd slept around, and he'd stayed away from other wolves. It had worked for him so far. That was, until he'd run into Wes, but he couldn't help that.

That was completely out of his control. He wasn't upset about helping another wolf, though. In fact, this was helping Joseph.

He still felt guilty about having left Maurice the way that he had. If this was the omega that he could help, then that was good. It would make his life easier. At least he thought so. That, and he couldn't bear the idea of sending Wes away to fend for himself when the danger facing him was so pressing and real.

Joseph wouldn't be there to defend him either. He couldn't be there. He knew better than to confront another alpha. That meant death—or at least some real, true pain—for at least one of them.

And it wasn't like Joseph wanted to claim Wes as his own alpha.

He just wanted him to be a person, have his own life. Do what he wanted. He didn't want to own anyone that didn't want to be owned. Wes was a little bit magnificent and the last thing that Joseph wanted to do was to stop that magnificence from manifesting. He wanted to help him be free, just like the way that Joseph had freed himself from the shackles of his destiny years ago.

But it was also clear that Wes didn't have a clue.

At least Joseph hadn't been this clueless when he had first left his pack. They were pretty normal, trying their best to slip through the cracks of human life.

Joseph had heard of packs like Wes', but they were a myth, a legend. They were barbaric and they were the stuff of legends. But he could see it in Wes' eyes.

He wasn't lying.

Joseph understood completely why Wes was so scared.

He was going to help him. Whatever reservations he might have had, the moment he thought about helping Wes, he realized that it was more important that he help Wes than do anything else.

It might be the most important thing that he ever do in his life.

If Wes managed to escape, where was he going to go? What was he going to do? Joseph didn't even want to think about it. The very thought of it made him sick to his stomach. He could be shot, or worse, imprisoned and studied.

Then his entire species would be at risk and not just the sweet young man in front of him. As defiant as he was, Joseph was pretty sure that it would break him.

It could break even the strongest of alphas.

Wes was still watching him curiously when Joseph cocked his head and smiled at him. "Okay, Wes," he said. "How much?"

"How much what?"

"How much did you have saved up?"

Wes looks at him for a second, clearly wondering if he should tell him. Joseph could tell that he was embarrassed of what the answer was.

"It's okay," Joseph said. "I promise I'm not going to judge you."

Wes laughed at that. "You should, because it's pitiful. I mean, it might be enough to start, but..."

"Wes."

"About two hundred dollars."

Joseph had to stop his mouth from dropping open. If Wes really thought that two hundred dollars was enough for him to get settled, then he really had a lot more to learn than Joseph had anticipated.

Joseph smiled at him, trying to hide the shock in his face. "Well," he said. "We need to do something about that too."

Chapter Five

Wes hadn't expected Joseph to be so nice. Even once they started talking, Wes was pretty sure that he was going to turn into a horrible person, or that he was going to shift into an alpha asshole.

But that wasn't what had happened at all. Instead, Joseph had offered to let him stay, and when Wes had asked how that would work, Joseph had said that he would give him work around the house.

He had also said that Wes could stay without paying rent, which had surprised him, but he appreciated it nevertheless. It felt a bit like destiny that Joseph's cabin had been the one that Wes had broken into.

If it had been anyone else's cabin, he doubted that they would have had the conversation that they'd had the night before, over Chinese food and coffee. God, even the thought of that... it was so foreign to Wes. This wasn't the kind of life that he'd led up to that point. Joseph had opened his eyes to so much more. It was kind of hard for Wes to process that this was what his life could be like and that Joseph would help him get there.

He smiled as he thought about Joseph, stretching as he got out of the guestroom bed. It was the nicest bed that he had ever slept in, and these were the nicest clothes that he had ever worn, though much like Joseph had said, they were too big for him.

Joseph looked around at his new room. It was also the biggest, nicest room he had ever been in. Back at the farm, he slept in the garage with at least one other wolf, because they didn't want him to run away.

He had been lucky the night that he'd managed to escape, because Alfonso and Robin had gone out on a date and they had sworn Wes to secrecy.

It had been perfect for him, though he couldn't help but wonder what Griffin had done to the two of them after the escape was discovered.

It was none of his business, he told himself as he walked around the room. The room was huge and facing the east, so he could see sunlight streaming through the windows.

The light was soft and everything about the place was cozy. He could imagine himself here in the long-term, but he knew that wasn't very likely to happen.

It was too nice to be a stepping stone, Wes thought with a sigh. This was the perfect place for him. He could already tell.

And the fact that Joseph was so nice, kind and sweet… well, that didn't make him feel like he wanted to move on. He knew that Joseph was just taking pity on him, but even then, his gratitude was winning over his pride.

Without Joseph, he didn't know where he would be.

Especially because of the discussion they'd had the night before.

Joseph had told Wes that all he had to do was repair some things, help with some fixtures, make sure that everything was finished up and ready to live in. After all, Joseph had explained, the house was still not quite finished.

There were a few things that needed to be done and Joseph said that he wasn't handy, so he would appreciate Wes' help. Wes was handy, and he was happy to help, considering what Joseph was doing for him.

Wes knew that his handiness was being used as an excuse, but it was a good one and he didn't mind it. As long as it meant that he got to stay there, Joseph could have told him anything and he would have done it, though it was probably best that Joseph didn't know that.

He sighed as he thought about him. He remembered focusing on those long, calloused fingers—his hands were big, and his skin looked soft, but the ends of his fingers looked like they saw a lot of use, and Wes wanted to grab them and feel them against his own. He wanted to put them on his face and feel the creases of his skins, the ridges of his knuckles.

He closed his eyes as he felt his cheeks redden, thinking about what else he would love to do with Joseph's fingers. He wanted to have them on his cheeks, he wanted to suck them dry until—fuck. He needed to stop thinking about it.

He was sporting a pretty obvious morning wood and he couldn't go out there with a hard-on, especially not in Joseph's pajamas. That would have been… weird.

Nothing was going to happen between them. There was tension, sure, but that was only the natural imperative. It wasn't because there was actually anything between them. It was just that Joseph was an alpha and Wes was an omega, so their bodies were betraying them.

Wes' body certainly was, though he was sure he had never felt this way about Griffin. Sure, he had wanted Griffin to have him, so that he could end up pregnant, but he didn't think about Griffin like this when he closed his eyes.

He didn't seek him out when his bed was empty in the morning. He couldn't remember what he had dreamed about, but he was reasonably sure that it had been about Joseph.

He couldn't afford to get obsessed with the man that was helping him by letting him stay with him. He told himself to get a grip and went down to the floor to do push-ups, hoping that they would kill his boner.

After twenty, he was pretty sure that he was presentable enough to go downstairs. There was only one bathroom in the cabin at the end of the hallway, near where Wes had broken the window.

He could feel the wind chill going through the wall when he had been sleeping there and he was sure that he was going to feel it now when he was taking a shower.

The fact that there was only one bathroom in the entire cabin was unfortunate, Wes thought.

They would have to share it, which Wes guessed Joseph didn't really appreciate.

There was something about having to share a bathroom with a guy that he didn't know that well. He had done it before with his family, and obviously, they relieved themselves by going outside and washing in the river when they had shifted.

But Joseph's existence seemed a lot more... human. And Wes really wanted to fit in. He didn't want Joseph to feel like he had made a mistake by taking him in, and he was going to do his best to make sure that Joseph didn't think that he was a freak.

Once he was ready and there was sweat on his forehead, he decided that it was time to go downstairs.

He could hear Joseph talking to Devin and he couldn't help but smile at the way that his tone shifted when he talked to his mini pig. He was normally so wise sounding, but there was something sweet about the way he talked to Devin Bacon, almost paternal.

He wondered what kind of father Joseph would have been, if he had chosen to go through with his alpha nature. He appreciated that he hadn't, though he didn't know much about him.

He smiled when he saw Joseph on the floor, Devin doing circles around him, wearing a different sweater this time.

"Good morning," Wes said with a smile.

Joseph smiled back at him, then went back to playing with Devin. "Good morning to you. Did you sleep okay?"

"Yes, thank you," Wes said. "Can I ask you something?"

"Sure," Joseph replied.

"How many sweaters have you knitted your pig?"

Joseph narrowed his eyes as he thought about it. "I don't know," he said. "At least twenty?"

"Twenty," Wes echoed.

"Yeah, so I knit him one for each season, and obviously the summer ones aren't technically sweaters," he said. "They're more like... capes."

"You knit your pig capes."

"He gets cold!"

"I'm not judging you," Wes said, biting his lower lip to stop himself from smiling. "I feel like you should do whatever you want to do."

"Of course I should," Joseph said, grinning at him. "I took up knitting because it was a way to learn how to relax. I felt myself getting really wound-up all the time, living among humans, not being able to be true to my nature. I needed to find something to do with my hands."

Wes watched him. He wanted to tell him that he didn't have to explain himself to him, but Joseph wasn't doing it because he wanted to explain himself. That much was clear from the look on his face.

He was enjoying this. Wes knew, instantly, that it was because he never got to tell this story.

He never got to talk about the things that he did to stop himself from exploding. Wes approached him and sat down on the floor in front of him, smiling as Devin darted in and out from between their legs.

"But it felt pointless to do it if it wasn't going anywhere," Joseph said. "I wanted what I did to go somewhere. I knitted myself a few hats, but I don't know, that wasn't very fulfilling. So then I got Devin. I thought it would be good practice to knit him some hats, but... it was harder than I expected. Then I got hooked on making him sweaters."

"And you've been doing it ever since?"

Joseph nodded. "Some people run," he said. "I knit."

"I like it."

"You do?"

"Yeah," Wes replied. "Maybe you can teach me one day?"

Joseph smiled at him, though the smile didn't reach his eyes this time. "Sure," he said. "That sounds good."

Wes could feel his expression cool. He didn't want to think about the fact that this was temporary even if that was reality. Every time that he thought about it, he felt a stab in his stomach.

"So," Joseph said, standing up. "Would you like some coffee?"

Wes nodded. "What time is it? There were no clocks in my room."

Joseph sighed. "You don't have a phone?"

Wes shook his head. "No," he said. "Never have."

Joseph seemed to think about that for a second. Wes didn't know what the look on his face meant, and he wasn't sure if it was pity or something else, but whatever it was, he was absolutely certain that he didn't like it.

He poured Wes a coffee, walked over to where he was, and put it in his hand. Wes felt his fingertips brush against his own and it made him shudder. It made him weak at the knees and he had to take in a sharp breath to stop himself from saying or doing anything that he might regret.

Joseph pulled away from him quickly enough that he didn't have time to make a fool out of himself.

He leaned against the counter before he spoke, and Wes couldn't help but stare at the way that his clothes were clinging to his body, He could see muscles and lines from which he probably should have been averting his gaze, but he couldn't help himself.

There was something magnetic about Joseph. Joseph seemed to know the effect that he was having on Wes, because he cleared his throat and turned his face slightly away.

His cheeks were red, or they seemed red, but that could have easily been Wes' imagination.

His imagination was leading him into some very dark places that were making his cock hard again. He couldn't afford to be hard around Joseph, so he also turned, and he tried to concentrate by drowning his feelings in his coffee.

Joseph didn't say anything for a while.

When they were both finished with the coffee, Joseph broke the silence. "I was thinking that today we could go to town and get some stuff."

"Town," Wes said, his heart beating fast in his chest.

It might have been because he knew that his pack was there that he was nervous, but they would never dare do anything during the daylight.

"Yes, town," Joseph said once again. "Because I need to go shopping, and I don't know, maybe we could stop for brunch."

Wes licked his lips. "You want to go for brunch with me?"

"Could be fun," Joseph said. "And I mean, we're already going to be there. We need to go get you some clothes, because I'm guessing that you only have the stuff on your back."

"I have a few other pairs of underwear, but yeah… not much else."

"I thought so," Joseph said. "And my stuff doesn't really fit you, does it?"

Wes smiled, despite himself. "I like wearing your clothes."

Joseph blanched at that and Wes was worried that he had overstepped his boundaries.

Of course he had made everything awkward, Wes thought, his heart in his throat.

After all, that was who he was, and it was easy to see that this arrangement wouldn't last. Joseph was far too good for him. He cared too much about him. He gave him too much credit. Wes didn't even know what he was doing. He was trying to get away from his pack but other than the actual escape, he hadn't given it that much thought, and that had come to bite him in the ass.

Though in a way, he supposed that he had been lucky. If Wes had ended up at another alpha's house... He didn't even want to think about that. The idea made him sick to his stomach.

When he opened his eyes and managed to look at Joseph again, he noticed that Joseph was staring at him and smiling, though he hadn't quite regained his coloring.

"You can't," Joseph said, his smile wavering only a little bit. "Look, the pig is already better dressed than I am. You can't take my clothes too."

"Will you knit me a sweater?"

Joseph rolled his eyes, but he threw his head back and laughed. Wes loved the way that his laugh sounded—deep, rich and masculine. Like mahogany.

"Maybe for your birthday," Joseph said. "But come on, let's be serious. We need to shop for a wardrobe for you."

Wes took a deep breath. He could feel himself wavering. He didn't want to go to town, though of course he wanted to be around Joseph. He also didn't want to stay there alone. It didn't feel right staying in Joseph's house without him after Joseph had walked in on him using it as his hiding spot.

It wasn't his house and he wanted to show Joseph that he knew that. Still, he couldn't help but shift his weight between his feet and look down at the floor as Joseph looked at him.

Joseph approached him, slightly, and Wes could smell his presence. He could feel it everywhere in his body. He could feel it pulsating to his fingertips, to the ends of his toes, to the top of his head. He could feel it in his tongue, coating his mouth like sweet, tangy, caramel coffee.

Joseph curled a finger and tilted Wes' face up. "What is it?"

"It's nothing."

"You can tell me anything," Joseph said. "While you're here, you need to feel comfortable talking to me, Wes."

Wes tried to swallow down the knot in his throat.

"Wes."

"I don't want to."

"It's okay," Joseph said. "You're safe here. I promise."

Wes shuddered, but he felt that Joseph was grounding him by touching his face, and he didn't want to pull away from him. "I'm just a little worried, I guess."

"What are you worried about?"

"Honestly? I'm worried about my pack."

Joseph got close to him, tilted his face up, and their gazes met for a second. Joseph's eyes were fire when Wes looked at him, and he was sure that whatever he said then would be the truth, and that Wes better believe him.

"I will never let them hurt you," Joseph said. "I will never let anyone hurt you again."

Wes nodded, but he felt the question leave his lips before he could stop it. "Why?"

Joseph removed his hands at that point, and Wes wasn't sure why, though he suddenly felt a little adrift.

Joseph cleared his throat and then looked away from him. "I, uh..."

He let the sentence hang in the air.

"We should go," he said. "Before traffic gets bad."

Wes nodded. "Sure," he replied. "Just give me a minute. I'll go get dressed and then we can go."

Chapter Six

Joseph wasn't sure what had gotten into him when he had held Wes' face and looked deep into his eyes. He had never felt quite as protective as he had right then. He didn't need to touch Wes to make his point. That hadn't been necessary. Yet he had felt so compelled, it would have almost been wrong to stop himself from doing it.

He didn't think that he would have been able to. Wes was sitting in the passenger seat of the wagon, looking out the window and grinning. His eyes were closed and his hair was swaying in the wind. He needed a haircut, probably, but Joseph was simply enjoying looking at him.

He liked the way that Wes looked when he was relaxed. His eyes were half-closed and his face looked like it wasn't tense. Joseph realized that it was the first time that he had ever seen Wes like this, without any worry lining his face. It was the first time that it occurred to Joseph that Wes was actually really young and that it was clear that he had no idea what he was doing.

He couldn't help but smile. He wanted to reach out and thread his fingers through Wes' hair, tell him that he needed a haircut, bring his face close to his own and kiss the top of his head. But he wasn't going to do that. He wanted to give Wes a choice, and he wouldn't have been able to do that if he felt like he was being pursued by the man who was giving him a place to stay, who was allowing him to stay away from his pack.

After all, he wouldn't have felt comfortable turning him down, and he was already trying to escape an oppressive alpha who felt like he was entitled to his body. Joseph knew that he wasn't entitled to anything.

Every time Wes laughed when he was near him, or that he spoke, or that their gazes met and neither one of them looked away, it felt like a privilege to him.

The day had been incredible, too, even though Joseph had spent way too much money, far more than he had anticipated. He didn't mind that Wes didn't have a job, and really, he would have needed to hire an outside contractor to do the work that needed to be finished anyway because other than knitting, Joseph wasn't any good with his hands.

He was clumsy for a wolf. He was good at making things easy to understand, concepts, which was the reason why he had gone into copywriting and then marketing.

That, and the ability to do it wherever in the world he chose. That was important too. More important than anything else.

They got to a stop sign and Wes opened his eyes, the little smile disappearing from his face. "Are we home?"

Joseph felt the word stab him in the stomach. He hadn't expected Wes to mention home like that. The word felt sweet in his mouth, sugary, and for some reason that Joseph couldn't quite think up, it had brought tears to his eyes.

Wes looked at him, cocking his head and frowning. "Are you okay?"

"Yeah," Joseph said. "Fine. Just, uh, still getting used to how cold it is up here."

"It's so cold," Wes said, hugging himself. "I'm looking forward to shifting tonight. It's so much cozier."

Joseph laughed. It was true that being a wolf was warmer, because of the fur and the fact that they could run further. There was also the meat consumption. Their bodies as wolves were more used to the cold than their bodies as humans.

Joseph continued looking at the road ahead. He didn't want to think about the fact that they would be shifting soon. They had discussed some boundaries but Joseph couldn't help but still be a little worried. After all, he was able to resist the omega's scent when they were in human form, but he wasn't sure that he was going to be able to resist it when they were wolves.

"We need to talk about that," Joseph said as he pressed down on the gas.

Wes nodded. "I figured."

"Listen," Joseph said. "I know that tonight is going to be… different. I trained myself to ignore Devin, but—"

"I'll go into the woods."

"And your pack?"

Wes closed his eyes. "I would never want to hurt your pig," he said.

"Yeah, but you don't have to hurt yourself at my pig's expense," he replied. "We just need to come up with a plan. There is a basement in the cabin."

"A basement?"

"I know," Joseph said, shaking his head. "I know that it's not ideal."

Wes sighed. "It's okay."

Joseph watched him. "Really?"

"I mean, I get it," he said. "If I go out into the woods and my pack finds me..."

Joseph chewed on his lower lip. "What about the woodlands on the southside?"

"The ones past the lake?"

Joseph nodded. "They don't normally go that far, I take it."

"They don't," Wes replied. "But if they want to find me, and I'm by myself, I'm going to be shit out of luck."

Joseph nodded. He knew that Wes wouldn't be fast enough to run away from them. omegas weren't faster than alphas and they were almost never stronger. If Wes got caught by his alpha—whose name Joseph realized Wes hadn't told him—then he didn't think that he was going to be able to go back to Joseph's house.

He didn't want that.

The last thing that he wanted to worry about was Wes having to leave. He didn't want to think about what was going to happen to Wes when he returned to his original pack.

After all, there was a reason that Joseph had offered to let him stay. He had definitely meant that Wes could stay with him and he hadn't regretted it for a minute. If that meant that he would have to defend him from his alpha, then he supposed that was on him.

He would just have to make sure that he didn't fall into the trap of wanting to mate with him. He wasn't in heat yet—neither of them were—but the problem was that he liked Wes a lot and he could feel himself being drawn to him. But this was the reason he had trained so hard.

He hadn't decided that he would learn to stop himself from listening to his wolf instincts just to shoot down the first opportunity to do that. He needed to trust himself, but that was difficult around someone like Wes.

He took a deep breath before he spoke. "You're right," he said. "That's not good. If they find you, you won't be able to—"

"I know," Wes said. "I don't want to think about it. But shifting in a basement?"

Joseph bit his lower lip nervously. "I know," he said. "It would be cruel."

"But if it's what you feel that I have to do," Wes said, looking down at his lap.

Joseph looked at him for a second, at his shining eyes, at the way that his shoulders were slumping forward. He couldn't help himself, though he knew that he should have.

Wes looked up at him and smiled, though his smile didn't quite reach his eyes. "Okay," he said. "Then we'll go together."

"To which woods?"

"The ones across the lake," Joseph replied. "So that we're not accidentally ending up in their territory."

Wes' eyes widened as he took in that information. "I don't know, Joseph," he replied. "That sounds dangerous for you."

"You think I'm intimidating now? You should see me at night," Joseph winked at him. He hoped that he was coming across more secure than he felt, because this entire thing was throwing him for a loop. He wasn't sure how he was supposed to feel or why he was suddenly okay with putting all of his hard work at risk.

But Wes needed help and Joseph... well, he wouldn't have been okay with turning him down. He didn't think so, anyway.

Wes was watching him when Joseph caught him from the corner of his eye.

He turned slightly, just so that he could give him a reassuring smile, but Wes was frowning, a deep worry line creasing his forehead. "Are you sure?"

Joseph nodded. "Yes, because at least I can try to protect you then."

Wes continued saying nothing, which made Joseph feel like he needed to justify himself.

"Look, Wes, I would not feel okay with letting you go and shift by yourself, especially knowing that your pack might find you and drag you back with them. After all, there's a good reason that you're here, right?"

Joseph could see that Wes was biting the inside of his cheek thoughtfully. "Yes, but they might not."

"I know. But they might, too."

"But we can't know that."

Joseph nodded. "You're right. There's no way to know that, but there are ways to mitigate risk."

Wes nodded. "I guess that's true."

"And look, Wes," he said, his shaky voice a dead giveaway that he cared about this way more than he was supposed to. "If I never saw you again, I would never forgive myself."

Wes' expression softened and then he smiled at Joseph. "What about..."

Joseph chuckled slightly, shaking his head. "The other thing?"

When Wes spoke, his voice was so quiet that Joseph had to strain to hear him. "Yeah, the other thing." Joseph cleared his throat. He was trying to convince himself as much as he was trying to convince Wes, but there was no need for Wes to know that he wasn't nearly as sure of himself as he sounded.

"Well, I've been training for long enough that I think I should be okay, but if I'm not, I'll make sure not to spend the night at home."

"That makes sense," Wes said. "Though the last thing I want to do is drive you away from your home."

Joseph pinched the bridge of his nose. "It's just until we find a more permanent solution for you. For the time being, this makes sense, right?"

"Right," Wes said.

"Just make sure that you feed Devin when I'm gone? That fucker can hold grudges like the best of them."

Wes giggled. "Okay, got it. Feed the pig."

Joseph glared at him. "And he's not food."

"I know that."

"Do you know that at night?"

Wes opened his mouth in mock surprise. "I promise you," he said. "I'll keep my dirty paws off your pet pig."

***

Before either one of them knew it, it was nighttime. They had spent so much time chatting, talking about whatever, and just enjoying each other's company, that Joseph had been surprised at how quickly night had fallen.

The days weren't that short yet, and in theory, they should have both been prepared for it to happen. Luckily, as it got dark, they still had some time to get ready.

They didn't turn immediately once night fell, because that would have been torture, but closer to midnight.

It was a guarantee that the humans would have already gone to bed and that the animals in the forest would be up and about, doing whatever they needed to do, so that the wolves could catch some prey.

Not that this was going to be a hunting trip. It was going to be an exploratory one, at least for Joseph, though he supposed that Wes might already know the terrain pretty well.

He looked at Wes, who was leaning against the car and looking up at the stars, his arms crossed over his chest. He couldn't see him that well with his human eyes, but he could smell him, and he liked the fact that he was close. It made him feel good, like maybe this would all be okay, like maybe going out together wasn't such a bad idea.

Of course he still felt a draw to him, but there was something so *pleasant* about him too that he just wanted to make him feel good, and he thought that even his wolf form would know that it would be better to leave him undisturbed.

He caught his reflection in the backseat's window and smiled at all the layers that he was wearing. He needed to start doing certain things to make the shifting process easier.

He sat down on the wet ground, which was uncomfortable on his denim clad ass, and started to undo the laces of his boots.

He looked up at Wes, who was looking down at him, doing nothing.

They were finally sharing something like a companionable silence after they had talked each other's ears off all day.

There was something that made the first shift of the year contemplative for everyone so Joseph didn't mind that they had both fallen quiet.

This was nice, though. There was certainly some anxiety, at least on Joseph's part, because the omega's scent was strong and he could feel it getting stronger as they approached shifting time.

He thought that he would be able to resist it.

He told himself that he had to, because Wes was counting on him, because Wes was living with him and the last thing that Joseph wanted to do was make him feel like he had to run away again.

"Excited?" Wes asked.

Joseph chuckled. "A little," he said. "More nervous than usual."

"Yeah," Wes replied. "Same here."

Joseph nodded, his heart leaping in his chest, and went back to undoing the laces of his shoes. He wasn't sure exactly what Wes did to prepare, but every single wolf had a different ritual before they were about to turn. It might have been something as simple as a prayer.

Some wolves liked to exercise and some liked to eat human food, like chocolate, or a snack. Some people liked to have a bath or a hot shower, though they frequently ended up bathing in a river too.

A lot of it was so that they could feel a little human after they have turned, because it was easy to let the animalistic part of themselves take over. There were two parts of them and they needed to remember that one part was just as important as the other.

Joseph's life was tightly calculated and he didn't mind letting go and being a wolf so much. He liked it, he looked forward to it, but Wes was a wildcard and he wasn't sure what he was supposed to do about him.

There was also the fact that they would have to be in front of each other while they stripped down to nothing. Most wolves got rid of their clothes before they shifted, because the shifting process could create snags and accidents, especially in clothes with a lot of zippers and buttons—so anything that they would have worn for the current weather.

"Cold spring, huh?" Wes said.

Joseph nodded. "Coldest I can remember."

"You get used to it when you live up here."

Joseph nodded. "Might take me a bit."

"Don't worry," Wes said. "It does get easier."

Joseph nodded again. "I hope so."

Wes edged a little closer to him, just enough that Joseph could feel his warmth. They were pretty close to each other, though, and Joseph didn't know how that would work once they were shifting, especially because they would have to take all of their clothes off, and that seemed like a lot.

Joseph was short of breath when he finally managed to start undoing the buttons on his coat. He normally took a little while to get undressed, but there was something frenzied about the way that he was doing this. He wasn't shy at all, because nudity was something that he had grown up around, but this nudity felt supercharged because Wes was there watching him, staring at him, his mouth half-open and his eyes wide.

He was sure that Wes was lusting after him too, though that could have just been the allure of the omega. The allure of the omega was strong, his scent was strong, and everything about him felt like it might be too much to resist, like maybe this wasn't such a good idea.

He couldn't back out of it anymore.

He had driven them there and he needed to see it through. He couldn't let Wes go at this himself. There was absolutely no way that he could let him shift alone.

He kept peeling off layers, revealing himself to Wes, who was watching him intently, and Joseph noticed, not taking off any of his clothes. He was so gorgeous like this, when he was leaning against the car looking almost casually at him, that Joseph could feel his cock growing in his jeans.

He wasn't sure that he wanted to have an erection when he first got naked in front of Wes, but he thought that Wes would understand. This wouldn't be his fault, it would just be nature, and Wes would get that it was his scent that was drawing Joseph to him, that was making him rock hard when he thought about him.

He started to undo his clothes even more quickly and now his nails were getting caught on things and he was panting, but it didn't matter. He wasn't sure what was going on—though he had the vague idea that it had to do with shifting as much as it did with Wes—but he needed to disrobe, needed to get rid of everything constraining him so that he would be able to reveal himself to Wes more quickly.

That suddenly seemed like the most important thing to do.

Wes turned to watch him, still saying nothing, though Joseph could hear that his breath had quickened, could smell his scent. Joseph removed his shirt and then he was down to his underwear. If anyone else had seen him in that second, he would have probably looked like an idiot, but from the way that Wes was staring at him, he didn't feel like one at all. He felt... hot. Not just desired, and not just warm, but like every part of him was filling up with heat. The cold that surrounded them had stopped mattering. All that mattered was how warm he felt, the way that his heart was leaping in his chest, the way that the warmth was spreading to the ends of his fingertips.

He groaned, throwing his head back slightly. It was clearly sexual, but this was just a sexually charged situation and it didn't mean that anything had to happen between them. If this was all that happened between them, Joseph thought that might have been okay.

Maybe he would have been able to deal with this and just this. This didn't mean anything, it wouldn't necessarily lead to anything. This was just a ritual. They were getting ready for shifting.

Everything was still okay. They hadn't touched, hadn't kissed; they hadn't even exchanged any words, but Joseph knew that the tension wasn't in his head. When an omega got aroused, his scent became stronger and stronger, and now it was all that Joseph's nose could detect.

There was no mistaking that the musky, masculine scent that Wes was radiating was arousal, and Joseph felt it calling to him, like a magnet.

Wes was still watching him, and then he crossed the space between them and extended his hand. He didn't touch him—his fingertips hovered just above his skin, so he could feel their warmth, but he couldn't quite feel his touch.

Joseph swallowed. "Touch me," he said, his voice sounding strangled. "Please."

Wes didn't need to be asked twice. He groaned too and he closed the space that had been left between his fingertips and Joseph's chest.

Joseph chewed on his lower lip, trying to stop himself from screaming. It was just his fingers and he already felt like warm cosmic energy was spreading from where Wes had touched him to the rest of his body, and it was making his cock harder than it had been before, which Joseph hadn't even thought was possible.

Wes groaned and threw his head back, his eyes rolling to the back of his head. Joseph could see how turned on he was. He wanted to grab him by the waist and kiss him roughly on the mouth, but Joseph could feel his body starting to shift.

He could feel himself getting smaller, feel his muscles contracting, his bones burning. He took a deep breath and tried to steady himself as he felt everything crunching.

The shifting process always hurt, but Joseph was used to it. He didn't think that shifting this time was going to be that different, but when Wes was staring at him, he felt far more self-conscious than he normally did.

Then he looked at Wes and Wes had taken off his clothes, practically ripped them off, and he looked fucking gorgeous when he was naked, with washboard abs and muscled legs.

Then he moved away and leaned forward so that his legs were touching the ground, and Joseph closed his eyes, losing track of what he was doing. Shifting was always a personal ordeal and it took him a little while to find his bearings again when he was a wolf.

He whimpered, his paws against the wet ground, and he looked around, following Wes' scent until he found him behind the station wagon.

He ran toward Wes and Wes turned back, meeting his gaze, and running around him. Wes was a beautiful wolf with white and gray coloring and glimmering amber eyes.

He could smell him, and he was approaching him. Joseph jumped back and Wes jumped with him, encircling him, howling a little, then nuzzling into his neck. That was enough to provoke Joseph and the two ended up playing, their ears back, their jaw dropped. They sniffed each other's muzzle and tail and then rubbed themselves up against each other until they were both whimpering.

Wes and Joseph were both spent after a while and Wes nuzzled up to him, licking him on the muzzle, and then moving away from him slightly. Then he bowed his head down and offered his neck.

Everything in Joseph was screaming to take it. He wanted to, his instinct was to do it, but he didn't want to make Wes his omega. He wanted him to be independent, because clearly that was what Wes wanted for himself, and Joseph didn't feel like it would be a good thing to intervene.

He felt his human side winning out, which made him yelp—he wanted to take Wes, and the omega smelled so good that he needed to run away from him.

Wes was staring at him with those piercing amber eyes, his ears perked up. Clearly, he had picked up on the fact that something was wrong. Joseph understood that he needed to give him more, but he couldn't.

After Wes had wanted to submit to him, Joseph knew that he couldn't resist him anymore.

Yelping once more, this time toward the moon, he turned around and ran away from Wes. He could hear his howls, but it didn't matter.

He couldn't spend the night around him, no matter what.

Chapter Seven

Wes was disoriented when he got back to the house. He could track it, which wasn't a problem, and it wasn't that far. He hadn't detected the rest of his original pack—no, his only pack, because Joseph had rejected him and so his original pack was the only pack that he had ever known—which should have been lucky.

Except that he could only feel a pit growing in his stomach.

From Joseph's actions, it was clear that all Wes was to him was a charity case. He could have chosen to make him family, but that hadn't been what had happened at all. Instead, he had turned him down, every single wish that he had had to become Joseph's omega was shut down in an instant.

It hadn't taken Wes long to realize that Joseph would have been someone that he wouldn't have minded raising a family with. But a family wasn't the same as a pack, though for their species, the differences were intellectual only.

He had thought that everything was going well when they were playing with each other in that field. He could smell Joseph and neither one of them seemed to think that anything else mattered. He could tell from Joseph's scent that he was excited, that he was ready, that he wanted this. But even with all his allure, Wes hadn't been good enough for him.

He had shifted in front of the house, because he wasn't going to take Joseph's vehicle, and he hadn't had the foresight to bring his jeans in his mouth, so he was stuck outside of the cabin wearing nothing, feeling the wind chill seep into his bones.

He hugged himself. He was so cold. The window still hadn't been boarded up so he supposed that he could walk up in theory and break into the house again. Joseph had said that he was supposed to feed Devin Bacon and he thought that it was quite possible that he was going to catch his death of cold if he stayed out there for too long.

He hugged himself and started to walk toward the cabin. His human feet didn't like the ground at all, so he needed to get this done quickly, but the moment that he approached the cabin he was hit by the smell of an alpha.

His alpha.

Not Joseph's musky sandalwood smell, spicy and earthy. Griffin smelled like jalapeños and his scent made Wes' eyes water. He needed some clothes. He couldn't escape from this if he was butt naked but he couldn't exactly go in there and get clothes.

They were there. He could smell the rest of the betas, the rest of his pack, but mostly he could smell Griffin, and Griffin was angry. He looked around, wondering where Joseph was, wondering why he couldn't smell him.

He didn't have an alpha to defend him. It made sense that he was going to be dragged back to his pack—it made perfect sense that everything that he had tried to do would be pointless.

He had been deluded about being able to get away from his destiny.

And he needed to go in there and protect Joseph's pig. He was sure that his pack would already be tearing him apart if they had gotten to him. He would just offer himself to Griffin and make sure that any complication was gone from his life.

He took another deep shuddering breath. His eyes were practically full of tears when he approached the door and opened the handle.

He needed to be brave, but he could feel how hard it would be. He cleared his throat and screamed. "Hey, Griffin! I'm here now! Why don't you come get me?"

He could feel the scent getting stronger in the house. They were all already there, probably all in their human form.

He could hear footsteps approaching him. He had closed the door behind him, because he didn't want the cold to get in, but also because he didn't want Joseph to step in and have to fight the alpha in his house.

An alpha who shouldn't be there. Griffin should have known better than to be there, but he clearly wanted Wes as his prize, and he wasn't going to stop until he got him.

He could smell his scent getting closer.

Wes closed his eyes, waiting to be punched, but instead, he heard laughter. He opened one eye after another to see Griffin standing there, smirking at him.

Griffin was much taller than him, broader, but it was clear that they were related from the features that they both sported, especially their eyes. Sometimes, Wes thought that looking at Griffin's face was like looking into a mirror.

Griffin made a show of trailing his gaze over his body, stopping to look at his crotch. Then he took a step closer to him. He put his hand over Wes' shoulder and yanked him closer to him. "You," he said, baring his teeth.

Griffin's teeth didn't make him look sexy, they just made him look scary. Wes didn't want to spend any longer than he had to looking at them. He turned his face away.

"We've been worried sick about you," Griffin said, his voice a growl. Wes doubted that he was telling the truth, but he tried his best to stay where he was, not even taking a step back though his body was screaming to.

He was afraid of Griffin, but mostly, he was afraid for Joseph.

For reasons that he couldn't quite articulate, he realized that he was way more worried about Joseph than he was himself. For the first time in his life, he cared more about what would happen to someone other than himself if he remained there.

After all, he knew that being an Omega to Griffin would be bad, but he could already imagine something much worse. The worst part for him would be to watch Griffin destroy Joseph's life.

Wes closed his eyes, able to see exactly what kind of disaster Griffin would wreak on Joseph's house, on his life. No wonder Joseph hadn't taken Wes for one of his pack when he had offered.

It was too dangerous. An alpha didn't mess with another alpha's omega like that.

There was a reason why it wasn't done and that reason had become clear as day to him when Griffin was standing right in front of him, looking terrifying.

Joseph didn't deserve any of this.

Joseph was sweet and kind and good. Wes had to take responsibility for all of this, since it was, after all, his fault. He didn't have to go over there, he didn't have to break into Joseph's house, and he didn't have to bring Griffin into Joseph's life.

Joseph had tried so hard to be normal, to be good. And he had been, at least as far as Wes could tell, and Wes definitely admired him for that.

Wes liked Joseph and he wanted Joseph to keep everything that he had built for himself.

Maybe he more than liked Joseph. He closed his eyes. How he felt about Joseph wasn't at all relevant. It didn't matter, because soon, he would stop being in Joseph's life.

Joseph had changed him, he realized, as Griffin glowered at him. Until he had met Joseph, Wes hadn't come to realize that it was possible to be an alpha who was also a good person.

Now that he was standing face-to-face with Griffin, he knew that he had to get him out of there, that he had to get him away from Joseph's house and from Joseph's pet.

That he had to get him out of Joseph's life. That he had to make sure that Joseph was never confronted by this.

Though it hurt him to lie, he knew that he had to. It was the only way that he was going to be able to do what needed to be done. "I'm sorry," he said, every word sounding salty in his mouth. "I should not have run."

Griffin scoffed, getting close enough to him that Wes could smell his breath, that he could see the lines under his eyes. He could have been anything from forty to sixty years older than Wes and he wouldn't have known. Their pack never celebrated birthdays.

Wes didn't even know how old he was himself, though he had some understanding of it.

He had reached maturity, which was important, because that meant he could bear his alpha's children.

And like all of the other wolves that were now surrounding them knew, that was the important part of being an omega. Absolutely nothing else. "You shouldn't have," Griffin said. "You've misbehaved."

"I know," Wes said, swallowing when he said that. Fuck, he didn't want to think about what his punishment would be, though he guessed that it would be hard.

Griffin traced his jawline and then moved back, yanking his hair, and moving Wes' face very close to his own. Wes tried to swallow down the rock in his throat, his heart beating fast in his chest. He didn't know if he was going to get beat up on top of fulfilling his destiny—which normally would have made him shudder. There was no shuddering then, because he was so close to Griffin and he already knew exactly what would happen if he showed just how afraid he was.

Griffin delighted in it. He would make him feel the pain. He would make him understand just how stupid he had been to ever think that leaving was okay, that it was something he could have done.

Of course it wasn't something he could have done.

He couldn't believe that he'd been that stupid.

He opened his mouth, tears welling up in his eyes. "I'm sorry, Griffin," he said. He hated the way that Griffin's name sounded in his mouth. He wanted to spit out, tell him to never come near him again, get him away from Joseph's house and from his own person as quickly as possible. But, of course, he couldn't do that. He needed to act humble, like he was truly upset, because he knew where this would go otherwise. "I regret it."

Griffin let go of his hair and chuckled, throwing his head back. His voice was so gravelly. It threw Wes slightly off, the way that he was smiling, the way that he was looking at him.

Then Griffin started to circle around him. He was so close and Wes could smell his arousal, which made his stomach turn. "I see that the alpha here hasn't taken you."

Wes swallowed. Alpha traces could be smelled on omegas and since Joseph hadn't claimed him, then he had no excuse not to go with Griffin. "That's right," he said. "He didn't... I'm yours."

"That's what I like to hear," Griffin said. "Don't you know how much I missed you? I keep having to take others, but they're not worthy of me. And you smell so amazing now. I can't wait until you're in heat."

Wes swallowed.

"You're already so tasty," Griffin said. "Maybe I could take you right here and now. Bet you would love that, wouldn't you?"

Griffin ran his hands down Wes' back. He felt himself shuddering, but it wasn't a good type of shudder. He felt sick to his stomach. Griffin grabbed his ass, squeezed it, and then moved his finger down so that it was close to his crack.

"You can run all you want, Wes, but you don't fool me," he said. "You want this. You want to be my bitch, don't you?"

Wes closed his eyes. He didn't—he really, really didn't, but he knew that his body would betray him sooner or later, and Griffin would have his way with him no matter how much he pleaded.

"Please," he said. "Can we do this when we get home? Please?"

"Fine," Griffin said. "But you're nude and so ripe for the picking. What if we get one of the betas to do it? Get you warm and ready for me. How does that sound?"

Wes closed his eyes, tears streaming down his face. "Do whatever you need to do, Griffin."

"That's what I like to hear," Griffin said.

Wes tried not to sniffle. He knew better than to show his weakness in front of this wolf, but there was a part of him that wanted to drop down to his knees and beg Griffin to let him stay.

He wasn't even paying attention to all the betas that surrounded him, desire in their eyes. They would do whatever Griffin told them and though he was sure that a few of them felt a little sorry for him, it clearly wasn't enough to get any of them to stop.

Wes had reached his mature age and that meant that, just like any other beta, he was going to be initiated.

After all, they would all have a turn with him too, because that was the way that it worked in his pack.

Maybe it was not the way that it worked in other packs, but he had been told about this for years. He knew that for the next few weeks he would be little more than a fucktoy for his pack until Griffin decided that it was time to get him pregnant.

Since Griffin was the only one who could, he didn't care that all the other wolves had a turn. Wes was basically a rag, and eventually, the rag would give birth to a baby.

If the baby was an alpha, then Griffin would kick him out before he came of age. More likely, he would be an omega and then... fuck, Wes didn't even want to think about it. Maybe he would try to escape again when he had the baby, though that would probably be harder.

He swallowed, looking around Joseph's home, where Joseph had so kindly taken him in, even after everything that Wes had done.

The initiation was bound to happen and Wes knew that. He just wasn't sure when it would happen, and he would try to put it off as much as he could. "Can I get some clothes before we go?"

Griffin seemed to think about this for a second. "No," he said. "I like you like this. We all like you like this."

Wes closed his eyes as he heard the snickers of the other wolves around him. He could feel himself blushing, his heart dropping to his stomach. He needed to do this. He just wished it wasn't so fucking hard. "But Griffin," he said, trying to appeal to the alpha's rational side. "It's really cold outside."

"Yes, and you could be wearing your clothes, if you hadn't run off like a bitch"

"I'm sorry."

Griffin laughed quietly again. "You will be."

Wes felt his stomach churning again. He tried to think through the next few steps, what was about to happen.

If he just took everything a few seconds at a time, that might make it more bearable.

He turned around and started walking toward the door. The betas were quietly following behind him, though there were only a few of them there.

The threatening ones, Wes knew. The ones that Wes couldn't consider friends by any stretch of the imagination.

Their pack was small—only seven wolves—but there was only one omega, and it was clear that they all wanted Wes. The fact that he had thought he would have simply been able to leave wasn't just naïve, it was extremely stupid.

He couldn't believe that he thought he had found a way to get away from his alpha.

His alpha owned him and the idea that he might not was perhaps the most stupid one that Wes had ever had.

He could feel the tears stinging his face. The more boisterous they all got, the more desperate Wes felt.

Take it easy, he told himself. *You can do this.*

Just take it slow.

He tried to think about what would happen next.

He was going to be naked as he walked out the door and out of Joseph's live forever. He couldn't outrun his pack and he most certainly couldn't take them.

He tried to steel himself for both the cold and the humiliation. It was going to be hard, but they had to have brought a vehicle, because they lived too far away and from their place to the cabin was a two to three-hour walk.

He remembered that perfectly because he had done that very same walk only a few days ago, though his life felt like it was completely different ever since then.

Of course it wasn't, because now he was going back to it, and it didn't matter how he felt about it. He just knew that it needed to be done. He tried to count his blessings. They hadn't found Joseph's pig and they seemed mostly uninterested in his house. That was good, because Wes had a feeling that Joseph would have been devastated if other wolves had eaten his pet.

Maybe, if Wes got out of there quickly enough, Joseph would have fond memories of him. But definitely not if he let the rest of his pack eat Devin Bacon.

He wrapped his hand around the door handle to open it. He told himself that it would be okay, that this was what he needed to do for Joseph, that he was doing the right thing.

He couldn't stop it and that was probably a good thing.

He braced himself for the cold and turned the handle, the lock clicking at the same time.

The door was open and suddenly nothing made sense anymore.

The very moment that Wes opened the door, that was when everything became a blur.

He could smell Joseph, could see Joseph's shape, and then Joseph was in front of him, and Wes was surprised for a second that he hadn't smelled him before he had come in. He supposed that it was probably because he was so afraid, because he was going to have to leave with Griffin, and all that he could focus on was the way that Griffin smelled.

He only had a second to process everything. Then Joseph was shoving him aside, though not unkindly, in as much as one person could shove another one aside gently.

Wes still hit the wall and slid down, though he wasn't sure if it was because he was exhausted or because he had been pushed.

Then there was a skirmish, and Joseph had Griffin against the wall, and he was pounding on his face.

Red and Tom, the two betas that Griffin had brought along with him, were trying to get him off, grabbing at his hands, trying to move him by the waist. But they could tell that he was an alpha, and that if things went wrong, they would probably be beaten to a pulp.

That's why they weren't trying very hard, or at least that was all that Wes could surmise from his spot in the hallway. He felt very useless as he sat there, doing nothing, fat tears still sliding down his face. He was sitting on the floor, still completely naked, after having been knocked over when Joseph had run inside.

He still had Griffin pinned against the wall, his forearm on Griffin's windpipe, and Wes was both impressed and a little scared that Joseph was managing to dangle a man the size of Griffin by doing what he was doing.

"What the fuck are you doing in my house?" Joseph asked, baring his teeth.

Wes knew that was the first time that he had ever heard Joseph angry, and there was something powerful about his speech. His voice reminded him of how Joseph looked when he had shifted into a wolf.

He was imposing, scary, big. Griffin was scary too but in a different way. Wes had always thought that Griffin could beat any other alpha in a fight but it took him a little while to get his bearings.

He pushed back, hitting Joseph in the stomach with his knee, and both Tom and Red moved out of the way. Then it was Griffin who had Joseph pinned against the wall, though not nearly with as much raw anger as Wes felt Joseph had.

Joseph didn't take any time to get back at him. He kneed him in the crotch, which made Griffin double down in pain. It was a low blow, but Joseph was right to be angry—this was his house and there was no need for Wes' pack to be there.

Griffin was on the floor next to Wes, which made Wes scramble to get to his feet. The last thing that he wanted to do was be sitting right next to Griffin.

Joseph approached Griffin, looked down, and sneered at him. "Now," he said. "Let me ask you once again before I beat the shit out of you and then call the cops. What the fuck are you doing in my house?"

Griffin looked up at him. When he spoke, he was whimpering, which Wes could hardly believe. He had never heard Griffin whimper. He had never heard him afraid.

He could have kissed Joseph right then.

"I came to collect Wes. He's mine."

Joseph scoffed. His boot-clad foot was very close to Griffin's face and Wes was almost sure that Joseph would have happily hit him repeatedly in the face with it.

"Wes doesn't belong to anyone," Joseph said, his boot hovering over Griffin's face.

Griffin bared his teeth at him. "Wes is mine."

"Wes is no one's," Joseph replied. "And he's not going anywhere."

Wes was watching the two of them, his eyes wide. He wasn't sure what he could do about this. He knew better than to get between two alphas, but he wanted to help Joseph if he could.

He didn't think that was he was going to have to until he saw Griffin reaching for something in his back pocket. Wes knew that Griffin always carried a pocket knife with him and he wasn't okay with Griffin escalating things like that.

He certainly wasn't okay with Griffin hurting Joseph. He didn't think about it. He threw himself around Griffin, trying to tackle him to the ground. Then Griffin stood up, though Wes was wrapped around his waist and he was pushing him back, hitting himself up against the wall, but Wes had managed to get his pocket knife out of his pocket before he managed to use it.

He handed it to Joseph, who was staring at him wide-eyed, and then everything went black.

Chapter Eight

Joseph watched Wes. He had finally fallen asleep and he looked almost peaceful.

He was wearing pajamas that Joseph had bought him with Joseph's shirt, because it smelled like him, Wes had said, and he wanted something to ground him.

Joseph had run his hands over his hair and nodded, because of course that was okay. Anything that made him feel safe and grounded was okay.

That was all that Joseph wanted now, to make sure that Wes knew that he was going to be okay no matter what.

That was why he sat at the edge of the bed, still keeping watch on him, but saying nothing.

He didn't want to wake him too often, but it was important to make sure that he didn't sleep for too long because he might have had a concussion.

Joseph knew that Wes wouldn't want him to go to the hospital, but he was tempted to anyway. Yet, every time that Wes opened his eyes, he begged Joseph not to take him, though he expressed concerned for what might have happened to Joseph.

Joseph was fine. A little worse for wear, but nothing that he couldn't handle. Once Griffin had been disarmed and Joseph had his phone out of his pocket, Wes' original pack had backed down almost immediately.

They were very few things that wolves were afraid of as much as law enforcement. After the fight was over, and Joseph had threatened to call the police, Wes hadn't woken up. Joseph wasn't sure if it was because he was exhausted or because he was hurt, but there was nothing that he could do about it right then either way.

At the end of the fight, Griffin had challenged him, and they were going to have it out that night. Joseph wouldn't claim the Omega for himself if he won him from the other alpha, but he would at least try to free him so that he could go do whatever he wanted.

He closed his eyes as he remembered what he had walked in on. He didn't know how he felt about it. It was a mix of burning hot anger at what Wes had been subjected to and sadness that it was what he had running away from when he had stumbled into Joseph's home. When he had first gotten in the house, he could smell the fear along with the arousal in the air, but when it came to Wes's scent, Joseph had been able to tell right away that he was terrified.

It had done more than just upset him, because Joseph knew that it was his fault that it had gotten that far in the first place.

He should have never gone off by himself, and he should have never let Wes go off by himself either. He should have bit his neck, if that was what was going to protect him from that horrible pack.

He had thought that Wes would be okay, but he had been wrong. He thought that he would have been there to protect him in case that something did ever happen, but he had been wrong about that too.

Wes hadn't been protected at all, even though Joseph had promised that he would do it, and because of that, he had almost paid dearly.

Now it was daylight, and there were only a few hours left to go, and Joseph wasn't sure when Wes would seriously wake up, but he wasn't willing to leave his side.

They were in Joseph's bedroom, because Joseph didn't feel good about leaving Wes in the guest bedroom after what had happened.

He was sitting at the edge of the bed, looking at Wes, wondering what they would do after the fight happened. He had never tried to take over another alpha's pack before. Joseph knew that he was strong, and he was a good wolf, who seemed to be younger and faster than the alpha from Wes' original pack, but he might not be good enough for this.

His chief concern was that Wes was extremely valuable to his original pack, because once a pack lost an omega, they would never recover him. He knew that meant that the alpha would give it everything that he had so that the pack could keep Wes.

Joseph didn't want to think about the possibility that he would have to give Wes back if he lost, though Wes hardly belonged to him. Those were just the terms that he had agreed to so that he could get those wolves out of his house as soon as possible.

But he didn't think that he was going to lose.

He couldn't think that he was going to lose.

If he lost, there was no chance that he was handing Wes over. He would go against code, but he didn't care about that. He would at least fight until the end to provide Wes the ability to escape.

Even if it meant sacrificing himself, he would allow him the opportunity to leave. He would give him all his stuff, so that he could take it all. He had savings. He had money and a few properties. Wes would be okay for a few months until he figured everything out.

All that he cared about was that he took Devin Bacon with him, because he couldn't imagine leaving his pig with no one to care for him.

Wes stirred and Joseph looked at him, a smile on his face. "Hey," he said. "How are you feeling?"

Wes shook his head, rubbing his eyes. He sat up. His hair was sticking to his face and his eyes were only half-open, clearly still sleepy, but at least he didn't look like he was in pain.

He set his gaze on Joseph before he spoke. "Honestly, I'm feeling a bit like a truck ran me over."

"That doesn't surprise me," Joseph said. "Do you want a cup of tea or something?"

"No, I don't—some water, actually, would be good."

Joseph nodded and set his gaze on the water bottle on the nightstand. Wes turned around to grab it and sighed, closing his eyes tightly. Even when he was stressed, Joseph could see how gorgeous he was. All that he wanted to do was protect him, make sure that he knew that everything was going to be okay.

Whatever was going to happen to Joseph didn't matter. Everything was going to be okay for Wes, whether he had to fight to his last breath to make it okay.

Wes took a sip of water, some dribbling down his chin. He removed the bottle from his mouth and closed his eyes. "I think I didn't realize how thirsty I was."

Joseph nodded. "That happens."

Wes set his gaze on him. "Joseph?"

"What is it?"

"I want you know that I'm okay," Wes said. He reached out and grabbed Joseph's hand. His hand was soft and warm against Joseph's and Joseph was a little startled at his touch.

"Good," he said. "I'm glad that you're okay."

They were quiet for a few seconds. Joseph spoke again, partly because this felt like goodbye. "I want you to know something too," Joseph said. "I don't think that I would be able to deal with it if you weren't okay. I'm sorry that I left you alone."

Wes furrowed his brow.

"I… I didn't want to do something which you wouldn't want in your right mind," Joseph said, trying to ignore the knot in his throat. "I thought that if I left you alone, that meant there was less of a chance of that. But I didn't realize just how vulnerable that would leave you. And I was wrong to do that."

Wes closed his eyes. "That's why you left?"

"Yes," Joseph said. "It wasn't because I didn't want to take you. I did. I really did."

"But you wanted me to be completely okay with it," Wes said, more to himself than to Joseph.

"It wouldn't have felt right if you weren't," Joseph said. "And the last thing I wanted to do was make you feel like you were trapped with me."

"I don't."

"You don't what?"

"Feel trapped with you," Wes said, squeezing his hand. Joseph smiled at him. He brushed his hair away from his face and got a little closer to him, mostly to tell him that everything was going to be okay. But he didn't do that. Instead, he looked into his eyes as Wes continued talking. "Thank you, so much, for everything you did for me yesterday."

Joseph chuckled, shaking his head. "It wasn't yesterday."

Wes scoffed. "Of course it was."

"It really wasn't." Joseph said. "Do you know what year it is?"

"Of course I know what year it is. I'm not an idiot," Wes said.

Joseph smiled. "I know you're not an idiot. I was worried that you were hurt."

"I'm not hurt, either," Wes said. "Thanks to you."

Joseph smiled. He was going to tell Wes all about Griffin's challenge, but he didn't want to quite yet. Wes got closer to him and planted a kiss on his mouth, his lips soft and warm against Joseph's. The kiss shouldn't have taken him by surprise, but it did anyway, and his heart was beating fast in his chest when Wes pulled away from him.

Joseph opened his eyes, setting his gaze on Wes' face. "What was that for?"

"Everything," Wes said. "And I want you to understand something, too."

"What?"

"You," he said. "I want to be part of your pack."

Joseph shook his head, a little sadly. "Wes, I don't have a pack."

"But you could," Wes said. "Or at least a family."

Before Joseph could think of anything to say, Wes' lips were on his again. He didn't resist, because this was exactly what he wanted, and he didn't realize just how much he had wanted it—though his body certainly did—until Wes was kissing him on the mouth, and he was opening his lips to let him in.

Wes was a good kisser, but there was more than that there. There was a sort of quiet desperation that had been simmering close to the surface from the beginning, from when they had first met, so even if Joseph wanted to stop this from happening, he didn't think that he could.

But there was no part of him that wanted to stop it, either. He pressed his face up against Wes', letting the kiss get faster and faster until Wes was laying on his back in the bed again and Joseph was on top of him, breathing so quickly that he felt like it was making him dizzy.

He moved his face away from Wes' for a second. "Are you sure about this?"

"More certain than I have been of anything else in my life," Wes said, just as breathlessly.

Joseph smiled at him. Wes smiled back, his hazel amber eyes glimmering.

Joseph brushed the hair away from his face and kissed him on the mouth again. They spent a long time like that, Joseph on top of him, simply making out with him and doing little else, though every fiber of his body screamed to take it further.

He stopped kissing him when even that felt like too much. His cock was harder than it felt like it might have ever been in his entire life and he was pretty sure that if he kept going for too much longer he would have come.

He wanted to come, but not yet.

He moved his hand down, slowly, so that Wes could feel him stroking him over the thin fabric of his pajamas. Wes threw his head back and gasped, his entire body shuddering, and Joseph felt like he could come just from looking at him.

"I want to take your clothes off," Joseph said.

Wes' eyes fluttered open and he set his gaze on Joseph. "Only if you take your clothes off first."

Joseph smiled. He sat up slightly so that he could take off his shirt and then Wes reached over so that he could fumble with the buttons on Joseph's jeans. Joseph groaned when Wes moved his jeans down so that his fingernails scraped against his skin, ever-so-slightly, just enough to make him shiver and to make him keenly aware that he was there, that Wes was under him, and that Wes was licking his lips when he was setting his gaze on Joseph's erection.

"Take those off," Wes said.

Joseph nodded. He had to move in a slightly awkward way to make sure that he could take off his boxers, but regardless of how ungracefully he moved, Wes still seemed to be looking at him with what Joseph could only have described as desire.

It made him even harder—his cock was throbbing by the time that he managed to take off his boxers and throw them on the floor somewhere around the bedroom.

He wasn't sure where they had gone and he didn't particularly care. He just knew that he wanted to keep kissing Wes until he ran out of breath. That was the most important thing that he could do. But Wes grabbed his cock, firmly, and his hand was perfect on Joseph's erection. He moved his hand up and down, not much, just a tease—grabbing the head of his cock, stimulating the most sensitive part of it.

Joseph threw his head back and moaned.

"I love your dick," Wes said. "I've been wanting to do that ever since the first time I saw you naked."

Joseph groaned again. He wanted to answer, but he seemed to have forgotten the ability to speak.

Wes laughed. "I'm going to take that as a yes."

Joseph didn't say anything, he just watched as Wes moved so that his face was level to Joseph's crotch. He wrapped his gorgeous lips around Joseph's cock and looked up at him as he moved his lips back and forth over his hardened dick, still holding Joseph's gaze.

"No," Joseph said, putting his hand on Wes' head.

Wes stopped.

Joseph shook his head. "I want to come inside of you," Joseph finally managed to say in between pants. Carefully, Wes removed his cock from his mouth, licking his sensitive head, lapping up his precum, and then he moved away from him, taking off his clothes desperately, until he was naked in front of Joseph.

Joseph looked at him, his eyes wide. "Has anyone ever told you how gorgeous you are?"

Wes smiled. He took off his boxers, threw them somewhere in the vicinity of Joseph's own, and lifted his knees to his chest. "I want you to fuck me."

Joseph groaned once more. He wanted to fuck Wes too, and he smelled so good, like sex, and like himself, and he really, really wanted to be inside him, probably more than he had ever wanted anything else in his life, but he knew the risk, though Wes wasn't in heat yet.

He nodded. "I'll get a condom—"

"No," Wes said. "I want you. All of you."

Joseph threw his head back and moaned. He was pretty sure that he could have come right then and there, but he was lucky that he didn't, because he lowered himself slightly and grabbed Wes by the waist, bringing him closer to him.

"I'm ready for you," Wes said.

Joseph groaned once more. Omegas were self-lubricating, and there was something particularly hot about entering him, which he did slowly and carefully, trying his best not to be too overwhelming for him.

Wes grabbed on to the sheets next to him.

Joseph moaned. "You're so fucking hot."

There was very little that he could do. He had already held it for so long, he didn't think that he was going to be able to any longer. Which was lucky, because he could see Wes' cock covered in precum, already looking like he was going to explode.

He grabbed Wes' cock and moved his hand up and down as he started to thrust his hips back and forth, hitting his sweet spot, watching Wes' face redden as he brought him closer and closer to orgasm. He matched the rhythm of his hips to the rhythm of his hand and then he closed his eyes as he felt the orgasm spreading from his core to the rest of his body, almost too much to handle, and then he was telling him that he was going to come.

He could feel his cock getting larger as he came, because Wes was an omega, and Wes set his gaze on

Joseph's eyes as he came inside of him, the entire thing was hot, all while his body made sure that Wes got every drop of him, every single part of him. The orgasm was too much, it lasted too long, it made his ears ring until he had to drop to Wes' side.

He was panting and Wes was panting, and then Wes slid his hand in Joseph's own and Joseph's heart leaped in his chest. The realization of what the two of them had done was just setting in.

"Can I offer you my neck now?" Wes said when they had both managed to catch their breath enough to speak.

Joseph closed his eyes. "Yeah," he said. "About that..."

Chapter Nine

Wes wasn't okay with the challenge, but there was nothing that he could do. He understood why Joseph had to challenge Griffin, but that didn't mean that he had to like it, and as the night grew closer, he grew more and more apprehensive.

He got that it was about more than just himself, but he wanted to believe that the two of them could have a nice quiet life without worrying about anything or anyone else. He wanted to believe that the two of them could simply be in this cabin, doing whatever the two of them wanted to do, having sex or hanging out with each other while Joseph knitted and Wes read.

But it wasn't as simple as that. He was still an omega, a desired one, and once a pack lost their omega, the pack was pretty much done for good. He felt a little bad about his original pack, but mostly, he was excited about possibly making a new one with Joseph. This was exactly what he had wanted all his life.

Without knowing it, Joseph had been exactly what he wanted. He didn't know just how much he wanted it until he knew Joseph, until Joseph was there, sleeping next to him, snoring a little bit.

He snuggled up close to him. He liked his warmth and he wished that there was anything that he could do to stop this from happening, but he wasn't going to wake him up and tell him that he couldn't do it.

On the other hand, he knew that the rest of his pack would start coming for him if they didn't do anything, and he really appreciated the fact that Joseph had decided to defend him, to try and claim him. After they were done having sex, Wes realized that he really did want them to be a pack, to be a family.

He never wanted to be away from Joseph again.

Joseph opened his eyes and looked at the clock on the nightstand. "It's time I get ready," he said, his voice coated with sleep.

"Okay," Wes replied. "Well, I'll get ready after—"

"No," Joseph said, his voice sounded more serious than Wes had ever heard it yet. He also sounded a little scared, but there was a chance that was all in his imagination. "You're not going to get ready. You're going to stay here, you're going to shift, and if I don't come back, you're going to run away. Do you understand?"

Wes closed eyes, shaking his head. "No," he said. He hated how whiny his voice sounded, but it didn't matter. He really didn't want this to happen the way that Joseph seemed to think that it would. "I'm not leaving without you."

Joseph scoffed. "I don't think you have a choice. You are going to leave without me if I'm not back or you go back to them. I will leave you everything. You will be set for a few months, enough to get yourself established. Enough to have a life as a person and not just an omega."

Wes closed his eyes, shaking his head. "That's not what I want."

"It's not what I want either," Joseph replied. "But it's something we need to think about. If I don't come back, you have to do what I say. I would never forgive myself if you were in danger because of me. Do you understand?"

Wes shook his head. "I can't stand the idea of being here without you. At least let me go with you, let me stay in the car. I'll shift then just watch and make sure to lock the door so that they can't come in."

Joseph watched him, saying nothing. "When I shift again, if I'm not yours, I will drive away."

"Do you promise?"

"I promise."

"You can't get medical attention for me. You have to go."

"I promise I won't, Joe."

Joseph nodded, very slowly. "Okay," he said. "Don't let me down."

"Don't worry," Wes replied. "I won't."

***

Wes could smell the fear in the air, though he wasn't sure if it was his own or Joseph's. He was peeking out the window, having already shifted, knowing that he couldn't leave this car even if he wanted to more than anything.

He howled when he smelled Griffin getting closer. He knew that Griffin and Joseph would go at it undisturbed, no betas around. Griffin would either kill Joseph or get him to submit if he won. Neither option was good. If Joseph won, he'd told Wes that he would make Griffin leave the two of them alone for good.

Their barbaric pack would come apart, too, because they wouldn't have an omega to torture.

He sought out Griffin. He couldn't see him very well, but he could smell him, and his paws scratched at the window, trying to defend his alpha—Joseph.

Joseph was an imposing wolf, but Griffin was just about his size, and for a second, Wes was very worried. The two of them circled each other for a bit until Joseph growled. That was all that it took—then the two of them were on top of each other, fighting, moving away for a few seconds, trying to get their bearings.

Joseph bared his teeth at Griffin, who tried to come at him again, but Joseph was faster than Griffin and managed to stay out of the way, his tail high in the air with confidence, his ears still perked up. The two of them yelped as Joseph managed to catch his neck, enough to make Griffin yelp and move around to try and get him off, but Joseph was too strong and managed to pin him to the ground. For a second, Griffin managed to slip out of Joseph's grasp, barking and yelping, attacking him by going around him and grabbing his tail, grabbing him enough so that Joseph was on his back.

Griffin jumped on him and grabbed his beck. Joseph's body writhed under him as he tried to free himself from his bite, Griffin towering over him.

Griffin looked like he was ready to snap Joseph's neck. Wes scratched at the window and howled again, fear building up inside of him as it seemed like Griffin had Joseph pinned down and Joseph wasn't going to get up again.

Griffin had him in his grip and Joseph continued to move. Griffin moved his body back by the scruff of his neck, his bite clearly powerful. He looked like he was about to snap Joseph's neck—like everything Joseph had warned him could happen, was just about to happen.

Then Griffin moved away from him for a second, to step on him, to snap his neck, and Joseph rolled away from him. It pissed Griffin off, Wes could tell it threw him off his game. Griffin approached him, head down, ears perked up, ready to take him head on.

Joseph whimpered, clearly in pain, but he managed to swing his head up and grab him by the neck himself, and then everything was a blur as the two of them engaged in a fight that Wes couldn't make much sense of from where he was standing.

He howled, unable to help himself, his paws scratching desperately at the window. He wanted to go help Joseph, to get Griffin away from him so that Joseph would be able to run away, but then Griffin was cowering in front of him, standing lower than Joseph and Joseph was barking at him.

Wes watched in amazement as Joseph barked at him, chasing him away from the woods, all while Griffin whimpered. Then Griffin looked back and scampered away.

Joseph turned back to him. He wasn't sure if Joseph could see him, but he could see Joseph, and he could taste the triumph in the air.

Joseph howled and Wes howled back.

Epilogue

It was late when Joseph woke up, and he thought he only did so because he could hear scrambling in the kitchen. He looked around, a little confused. He normally got up when it was still early in the morning, and his alarm guaranteed that he did when he didn't feel like it.

At some point, Wes must have turned his alarm off. He smiled as he thought about Wes, who he could hear whistling in the kitchen. It had been about a month since they had been official, seriously official. That very night, the very night that he had beaten Griffin, Wes had offered him his neck and Joseph had taken it.

That had made them family. There was also the fact that Wes was now in heat, so the two of them were fucking like there was no tomorrow, and being part of Joseph's pack allowed Wes extra protection. No one would try to take an omega away from his alpha.

That would have been certain death.

He walked down to the kitchen and looked at the scene unfolding in front of him. Wes was serving himself some coffee, reading a high school book because he had a GED test that afternoon, and Devin Bacon was at the feet of his chair, closing his eyes happily.

Joseph approached Wes and grabbed him by the waist, holding him close. "Good morning, gorgeous."

"Hi, Joe," Wes said. Joseph didn't allow anyone else in the world to call him Joe, but he melted when Wes did it. "I knew you didn't have to work today so I turned off your alarm. You have to get plenty of rest."

"Thanks," Joseph said, kissing him on the cheek. "That was very sweet of you, but there's a shit ton of stuff I have to get done."

"It can wait," Wes replied. He turned around and kissed Joseph on the lips. "Everything can wait."

Joseph took a second to drink this whole experience in. He took a deep breath and realized that something was different today. There was something else in the air, something sweet that he hadn't quite smelled before. He turned to look at Wes and Wes was smiling widely at him.

"Oh my God," Joseph said. "Really? Already?"

Wes didn't say anything and when Joseph didn't say anything else, he looked a little bit concerned. "I know. I know that it's a lot."

"It's not a lot," he said. "I'm sorry, I'm just surprised. Our lives are going to change with a cub."

"I know," Wes said. "Everything is going to be really different. I don't know if I thought it would happen this quickly but... I'm sorry."

"No, you don't have to apologize," Joseph said, kissing the tip of Wes' nose. "It's perfect."

Wes' eyes widened. "You really think so? It isn't going to be too much?"

Joseph smiled, shaking his head. "It's probably going to be too much, but that doesn't mean I don't want to do it."

Wes nodded, biting his lower lip. "There's something else."

"What's the matter?" Joseph said.

Wes didn't look at him when he answered. "I know that you and me are kind of together but I'm still an omega first and foremost—"

"Wes—"

"And I understand that I can never run away from that. It's who I am. You decide how to structure this pack so if what you want is--"

Joseph put his hand over Wes' mouth and shook his head, smiling at him. "Stop speaking. Right now, before you piss me off, or I'll have to spank you later."

Wes laughed a little and Joseph stepped away from him.

"Yeah, that would be terrible."

Joseph winked at him, but then he got serious. "You're not an omega, Wes. You're my partner. For good. My equal partner. We decide how we structure this family, not just me."

"Really?"

"Yes," Joseph said. He walked over to the pantry, to where he had hidden the ring that he had bought on a whim a few days ago. He hid it behind his back. "This is something that I wanted to do for a while, but I didn't want to put you off yet because I know it's a lot too."

Wes watched him. "What are you talking about?"

"How does Weston Turner sound?"

Wes' eyes widened. "For the cub?"

"No, silly," Joseph said. "For you."

He revealed the ring and Wes' eyes widened. He kissed him, jumped on him, hung from his waist, and kissed him again and again as the two of them danced around in their kitchen between giggles, until Joseph had to look at him very seriously. "So," he said. "Is that a yes?"

"Yes," Wes replied. "A hundred percent it's a yes."

"Good," Joseph said. "Now get off me. You have to study, don't you?"

"But I wanna hang out with you," Wes said, pouting.

"Don't worry," Joseph replied. "Devin and I will both be there. After all, I have a sweater to knit."

Printed in Great Britain
by Amazon